Meet the indomitable
CHARLIE M...

"One spook who actually becomes more appealing as he switches from apparent underdog to a very dangerous hound indeed . . . A splendidly simple trick denouement."　　　—*Kirkus Reviews*

"He pulls off what surely is one of the most outrageous, richest, and most delicious and satisfying comeuppances an underling has ever paid his superiors."　　　—*Buffalo News*

"All the ingenuity of James Bond at his best . . . The smash-surprise ending would send Ian Fleming into roars of laughter and applause."　　　—*Metro Magazine*

"Fine dialog, a tidy and cunning story, and one of the most surprising turnabouts of any ending in the espionage field make this one a pure delight."　　　—*Chicago Tribune*

"Spy readers will be cheering . . . A clever plot—and Charlie M—make this novel highly readable."　　　—*The Booklist*

Charlie M

Brian Freemantle

BALLANTINE BOOKS • NEW YORK

This novel was published in the United Kingdom as *Charlie Muffin*.

Copyright © 1977 by Innslodge Publications Ltd.

All rights reserved. Published in the United States by Ballantine Books, a division of Random House, Inc., New York.

Library of Congress Catalog Card Number: 77-75383

ISBN 0-345-30611-2

This edition published by arrangement with Doubleday & Company.

Manufactured in the United States of America

First Ballantine Books Edition: February 1980
Second Printing: December 1982

For *Algy* and *Gerry*,
for so many things

1

Like tombstones of forgotten graves, the decayed apartment buildings in the Friedrichstrasse pooled haphazard shadows in the approaching dusk and both men expertly used the cover, walking close to the walls. Although together, they carefully avoided physical contact and there was no conversation.

They stopped just before the open-spaced, free-fire area leading to Checkpoint Charlie, the taller, younger man using the pretence of taking a light for his cigarette from his companion to gaze over the outstretched arm towards the crossing point into West Berlin. On either side of the road, the criss-cross of tank traps indicated the limits of the minefield.

"Looks all right," he said, shielding the cigarette in a cupped hand. He was shaking, saw Charlie Muffin.

"It would, wouldn't it?" Charlie said dismissively.

Brian Snare managed to intrude his irritation into the noisy inhalation. The damned man never stopped, he thought.

"There's not the slightest sign of activity," insisted Snare. The wind drove the wispy fair hair over his face. Quickly he brushed it back, carefully smoothing it down.

"Don't be stupid," said Charlie. "Every border from the Baltic to the Mediterranean will be on full alert."

"Our documents are in order."

"So were Berenkov's. And I got him."

Snare looked from the border to the other man, arrested by the "I." Muffin had co-ordinated Berenkov's capture, probably the most important single spy arrest in Europe since the Second World War, and was frightened the credit for it was being taken away. Silly old sod. Another indication that he was past it, this constant need to prove himself.

"Well, we can't stay here all fucking night. Our visas expire in eight hours."

The carefully modulated obscenity sounded out of place from the Cambridge graduate. Had there still been National Service, thought Charlie, Snare would have rolled his own cigarettes in the barracks to prove he was an ordinary bloke and made up stories about NAAFI girls he'd screwed. No he wouldn't, he corrected immediately. The man would have used his family connections to obtain a commission, just as he was invoking them to push himself in the service. He'd still have lied about the NAAFI girls, though.

"Harrison crossed easily enough," argued Snare.

Three hours earlier, from the concealment of one of the former insurance office buildings further back in Leipzigerstrasse, they had watched the third member of the team, Douglas Harrison, go through the checkpoint unchallenged.

"That doesn't mean anything," dismissed Charlie. The habit of the other two men to address each other by their surnames irritated the older man, in whose world partners upon whom your life depended were called by their Christian names. He knew they used the public school practice to annoy him.

"You mean mates," Harrison had sneered when Charlie's anger had erupted months ago, at the start of the operation that was concluding that afternoon.

Like so many others, he'd lost the encounter, he remembered. The ill-considered retort—"I'd rather have a mate than a rich father and a public school accent"—had been laughed down in derision.

"I wouldn't, Charles," Snare had replied. "But that's not the point, is it? Why ever can't you drop this inverted snobbery? We'll try hard to be your chums, even though you don't like us."

"We've stood here too long," warned Snare. It was his turn to cross next.

Charlie nodded, moving back into the deeper shadows. The other man's shaking had worsened, he saw.

"The car-crossing documents are in the door pocket," said Snare, who had driven the hired Volkswagen with Harrison from West to East Berlin a week earlier. Cuthbertson had decreed they separate to avoid suspicion, so Charlie had arrived by train. But Cuthbertson had ordered him to bring the car back.

"We'll be waiting for you on the other side," added Snare, attempting a smile. "We'll have a celebration dinner in the Kempinski tonight."

But first they'd ring London, Charlie knew, to get in early with their account of the completed phase of the operation. His part in the affair was going to be undermined; he was sure of it. Bastards.

"What about the rest?" demanded Charlie.

Again Snare allowed the sigh of irritation.

"The original documents are in the car, too," said Snare. "But that's almost academic. Harrison had photocopies and by now they're in the West Berlin embassy waiting for the next diplomatic pouch. That'll satisfy the court."

"You've got photostats, too?" insisted Charlie.

Snare looked curiously at the older man.

"You know I have."

For several moments they stood like foreign language students seeking the proper words to express themselves.

"All right then," said Charlie, inadequately. He nodded, like a schoolmaster agreeing to a pupil's exit from the classroom.

Snare's face stiffened at the attitude. Supercilious fool.

"I'll see you at the Kempinski," said Snare, feeling words were expected from him.

"Book a table," said Charlie. "For three," he added, pointedly.

Abruptly Snare moved off, head hunched down into the collar of the British warm, hands thrust into the pockets, well-polished brogues sounding against the pavement. A man assured of his future, thought Charlie, briefly, turning in the other direction to walk back up Friedrichstrasse into East Berlin. Of what, he wondered, was he assured? Not a damned thing, he decided.

Just before the checkpoint, Snare turned, a typical tourist, raising his camera for the last picture of the divided city. Through the viewfinder, he strained to locate the retreating figure of Charlie Muffin.

It took over a minute, which Snare covered by jiggling with the light-meter and range adjustment. Muffin was very good, conceded Snare, reluctantly. The man was moving deep against the protection of the buildings again: no one from the observation points near the Wall would have detected him.

A professional. But still an out-of-date anachronism, concluded Snare contemptuously. Muffin was an oddity, like his name, a middle-aged field operative who had entered in the vacuum after the war, when manpower desperation had forced the service to reduce its standards to recruit from grammar schools and a class structure inherently suspect, and had risen to become one of the best-regarded officers in Whitehall.

Until the recent changes, that was. Now Sir Henry Cuthbertson was the Controller, with only George Wilberforce, a permanent civil servant and an excellent fellow, retained as his second-in-command. So from now on it was going to be different. It was going to be restored to its former, proper level and so Charlie Muffin was a disposable embarrassment, with his scuffed suede Hush Puppies, the Marks and Spencer shirts he didn't change daily and the flat, Manchester accent.

But he was too stupid to realise it. Odd, how someone so insensitive had lasted so long. Snare supposed it was what his tutor at Cambridge had called the native intelligence of the working class. In the field for twenty-five years, reflected Snare, turning back towards the Wall. An amazing achievement, he conceded, still reluctantly. An exception should be made to the Official Secrets Act, mused Snare, enjoying his private joke, to enable Muffin to be listed in the *Guinness Book of Records,* along with all the other freaks.

Five hundred yards away inside East Berlin, Charlie turned from the Friedrichstrasse on to Leipzigerstrasse, feeling safe. It was important to see Snare cross, he had decided. From the shelter of the doorway from which they'd both watched Harrison go over, he observed the man approach the booth and present his passport, hardly pausing in his stride in the briefest of formalities.

Slowly Charlie released the breath he had been holding, purposely creating a sad sound.

"Just like that," he said, quietly. In moments of puzzlement, when facts refused to correlate, Charlie unashamedly talked to himself, enumerating the factors worrying him, counting them off one by one on his fingers.

He was aware that the habit, as with everything else, amused Snare and Harrison. They'd even used it as an indicator of character imbalance in discussions with Cuthbertson, he knew. And Wilberforce, who had never liked him, would have joined in the criticism, Charlie guessed.

"Because of Berenkov's arrest, every border station should be tighter than a duck's bum," Charlie lectured himself. "Yet they go through, just like that."

He shook his head, sadly. So a decision had been made in that teak-lined office with its Grade One fitted carpet, bone china tea-cups and oil paintings of bewigged Chancellors of the Exchequer staring out unseeing into Parliament Square.

Tit for tat.

"But I'm not a tit," Charlie told the empty doorway.

Charlie sighed again, the depression deepening. Poor Günther.

But he had no choice, Charlie reasoned. It was a question of survival. Always the same justification, he thought, bitterly. Charlie Muffin had to survive, no matter how unacceptable the method. Or the way. Everyone before Cuthbertson had realised that: capitalised upon it even. But Cuthbertson had arrived with his punctilious, Army-trained attitudes and preconceived ideas, contemptuous of what might have happened before him.

But he had been clever enough to realise the importance of Berenkov, thought Charlie, tempering the disparagement. That would have been Wilberforce, he guessed, asshole crawling to ingratiate himself, showing Cuthbertson the way. Neither had had anything to do with it. But three months from now, Charlie knew, the affair would be established as a coup for the new regime. Fucking civil service.

He was purposely letting his mind drift to avoid what he had to do, Charlie accepted, realistically. Charlie's first visit on the Berenkov affair had been more than a year ago, during the days when he'd been properly acknowledged as the leading operative.

It wasn't until much later, when the potential of the investigation had been fully recognised and there had been the changes in Whitehall, that Snare and Harrison had been thrust upon him. And by then it didn't matter because Charlie had established, unknown to any of them, one of the many lifelines along which he could claw to safety, fertilising the protective association with Günther Bayer, gradually convincing the dissident student who believed him a traveller in engineering components, that one day he would help his defection.

What had happened thirty minutes before at Checkpoint Charlie meant that day had arrived.

Charlie had two brandies, in quick succession, in the gaudy cocktail bar of the Hotel Unter den Linden before calling the memorised number. Bayer responded immediately. The conversation was brief and guarded, conceding nothing, but Charlie could discern the tension in the other man. Poor sod, he thought. Yes, agreed the East German quickly, he could be at the hotel within an hour.

Charlie returned to the bar, deciding against the brandy he wanted. Drunkenness didn't help; it never did. He ordered beer instead, needing the excuse to sit there, gazing into the diminishing froth.

Did personal survival justify this? he recriminated. Perhaps his fears were unfounded, he countered hopefully. Perhaps he'd end up making a fool of himself and provide more ammunition for the two men already in West Berlin's Kempinski Hotel. And if that happened, Bayer would be the only beneficiary, a free man.

He shrugged away the reassurance. That was weak reasoning: people died because of weak reasoning.

There had been other instances like this, but it had never worried him so much before. Perhaps he was getting as old and ineffectual as Snare and Harrison were attempting to portray him. Cuthbertson and Wilberforce would be eager listeners, Charlie knew.

Bayer arrived in a rush, perspiration flecking his upper lip. He kept smiling, like a child anticipating a promised Christmas gift.

The two men moved immediately to a table away from the bar, Charlie ordering more beer as they went. They stayed silent until they were served, the East German fidgeting with impatience. I bet he always hunted for his presents early in December, thought Charlie.

"You've found a way?" demanded Bayer, as soon as the waiter moved off.

"I think so."

Bayer made a noise drinking his beer. Snare would have been distressed, thought Charlie, at the man's table manners.

"You've got the passport?" asked the Englishman.

Bayer reached toward his jacket pocket, but Charlie leaned across, stopping the movement.

"Not here," he said, annoyed.

"Sorry," he apologised. "I'm just excited, that's all."

It was a good forgery, Charlie knew. He'd had it prepared months before just off West Berlin's

Kurfürstendamm, using one of the best forgers among those who made a business trading people across the Wall. It had cost £150 and Charlie had only managed to retrieve £75 back on expenses; even then there'd been queries. He'd make up on this trip, though.

"How can it be done?" asked Bayer.

"When I came in, a week ago, I used the railway," said Charlie, gesturing out towards the overhead S Bahn linking East and West. That *had* been the first indication, decided Charlie, positively: Cuthbertson's explanation about the chances of detection had been banal.

Bayer nodded, urging him on.

"But the samples were brought in by another traveller, by car."

Bayer frowned, doubtfully.

". . . but . . ."

". . . And he's gone back, on foot," enlarged Charlie. "The car is here and the crossing papers are in order."

Bayer patted his pocket, where the passport lay.

"There's no entry date," he protested.

Charlie slid a small packet across the table.

"A date stamp," he said. "From the same man that made the passport. It'll match the documents in the car perfectly."

Bayer reached forward, seizing the other man's hand and holding it.

"I don't have the words to thank you," he said. His eyes were clouded, Charlie saw.

The Briton shrugged, uncomfortably.

"You must have dinner with Gretel and me, tomorrow, when it's all over."

"Gretel?"

"The girl I'm going to marry. I've already telephoned, telling her something could be happening."

Charlie concentrated on the beer before him.

"Was that wise?" he queried. "The call has to go through a manned exchange to the West."

"No one would have learned anything from the conversation," assured Bayer. "But Gretel knows."

Charlie looked at his watch, wanting to end the encounter. Perhaps he *was* getting too old, he thought.

"You've got three hours," he warned. "And you'll need time to enter the visa stamp."

The other man was having difficulty in speaking, Charlie saw.

"You're a marvellous man," Bayer struggled at last, reaching over the table again.

Charlie shrugged his hand off, irritably.

"Just don't panic. Remember, everything is properly documented."

From the lounge, Charlie watched the student collect the hired car and move off unsteadily into the traffic stream. He stayed, staring into the beer, thoughts fluttering through his mind like the clues in a paper-chase, scattered pieces creating nothing but a jagged line. Reluctantly he rose, paying the bill.

He had waited for an hour in that familiar Leipzigerstrasse doorway when he recognised the number of the approaching Volkswagen. Bayer was driving with confidence, more used to the vehicle. He passed the Briton, unseen in the shadows, slowing at the border approach to edge dutifully into the yellow smear of light.

The sudden glare of the spotlight, instantly joined by others that had obviously been specially positioned, was the first indication, and later Charlie reflected that it had been a mistake, throwing the switch so soon. A professional would have managed to reverse, to make a run for it. The manoeuvre wouldn't have achieved anything, of course, because immediately State Police vehicles and even armoured cars swarmed from the roads and alleys behind, blocking any retreat. For a few seconds, the Volkswagen actually continued forward, then jerked to a stop like an insect suddenly impaled under a microscope.

"Stay there," said Charlie, opening his private conversation. "They'll shoot if you move."

The driver's door thrust open, bouncing on its hinges, and Bayer darted out, crouching, trying to shield his face from the light.

"Halt!"

The command echoed over the checkpoint from several amplifiers. On the fringe of the illumination, Charlie could detect a frieze of white faces as the Americans formed to watch from their side of the border. Would Snare and Harrison be there? he wondered.

Bayer began to run, without direction, plunging towards the mines before realizing the error and twisting back to the roadway.

"Blinded," Charlie told himself.

"Halt!"

Louder this time, with more amplifiers turned on.

"Stop, you bloody fool," intoned Charlie.

Bayer was running back towards East Berlin now, towards the road-blocks he couldn't see, head thrown back, eyes bulging.

In the report to Cuthbertson two weeks later, Charlie wrote that those first shots were premature, like the lights, but by then the hysteria would have been gripping everyone. Given the lead, there was firing from all sides, even from the armoured vehicles towards which the student was fleeing. Bayer was thrown up by the crossfire, his feet snatched from the ground and then he collapsed, flopping and shapeless, like a rag-doll from which the stuffing had escaped.

The Volkswagen was sprayed in the shooting, too, and a bullet must have entered the petrol tank, which exploded in a red and yellow eruption. Debris fell on to the body, setting some of the clothing alight.

It took Charlie ten minutes to reach Bahnhof Friedrichstrasse and the train arrived almost immediately.

I'd have liked to see the Reichstag in Hitler's day, thought Charlie, as the train carried him to safety past the silhouette. By the time he'd reached Berlin it had been 1956 and most of the landmarks were skeletons of brick and girders. Günther's father had been a tank commander in a Panzer division, he remembered the student telling him: he carried a yellowed, fading picture in his wallet and was fond of producing it. Poor Günther.

The crossing formalities were brief and within thirty minutes he was disembarking at Bahnhof Zoo, selecting the main station because the crush of people would have confused any East German sent in immediate pursuit when they discovered their mistake.

He bathed leisurely at the Kempinski, even waiting while his second suit was pressed, enjoying the thought of the confrontation that was to come.

Snare and Harrison were already in the bar, both slightly drunk as he had anticipated they would be. Snare saw him first, stopping with his hand outstretched towards his glass.

"Oh my God," he managed, badly.

Harrison tried, but couldn't locate the words, standing with his head shaking refusal.

"You're dead," insisted Snare, finally. "We saw it happen."

And stayed quite unmoved, guessed Charlie. They really *had* tried to set him up.

"Brandy," he ordered, ignoring the two men. He made a measure between finger and thumb, indicating the large size to the barman.

Snare and Harrison really weren't good operatives, decided Charlie. No matter what the circumstances, they shouldn't have permitted such reaction.

"So you're having a wake for me," he suggested, sarcastically, nodding towards the drinks. He raised his own glass. "To my continued good health."

Both grabbed for their glasses, joining in the toast. Like hopefuls in a school play, thought Charlie, watching the performance.

They were losing their surprise now, recognizing the stupidity of their response and embarrassed by it.

"Charles," said Snare. "This is fantastic! Absolutely fantastic!"

"I thought you'd be pleased," goaded Charlie. "Booked a table for the celebration?"

"But we thought you'd been killed," said Harrison, speaking at last. He was a heavy, ponderous man, with a face that flushed easily beneath a disordered scrub of red hair and with thick, butcher's fingers. A genetic throwback, Charlie guessed, to a dalliance with a tradeswoman by one of his beknighted ancestors.

"Better fix it then, hadn't you?" replied Charlie.

"Of course," agreed Harrison, flustered more than Snare by the reappearance. He gestured to the barman to inform the restaurant.

"How did you do it, Charles?" asked Snare. He was fully recovered now, Charlie saw. They'd have already informed London of his death, Charlie knew. That had been the main reason for delaying his entry into the bar, to enable them to make every mistake. Cuthbertson would have told the Minister: the two would get a terrible bollicking.

Charlie waited until they had been ushered into the rebooked table and had ordered before replying.

"A bit of luck," he said, purposely deepening his accent. He paused, then made the decision.

". . . There was this mate . . ."

". . . who . . . ?" broke off Harrison stupidly.

Charlie considered the interruption for several minutes, robbed of the annoyance he had hoped to cause the other two men.

"His name was Bayer," he said, seriously. "Günther Bayer."

The waiter began serving the oysters, breaking the conversation again. Charlie gazed out of the restaurant window at the necklace of lights around the city. Somewhere out there, he thought, was a girl called Gretel. She wouldn't know yet, he realized. She'd still be preparing her own celebration meal.

"Tabasco?" enquired the waiter.

"No," answered Charlie, smiling. "Just lemon."

2

The grilled, narrow windows of the special interview room at Wormwood Scrubs were set high into the wall, making it impossible to see anything but a rectangle of grey sky.

Charlie gazed up, trying to determine whether it had started raining. He could feel the edge of the matting through the sole of his left shoe; if the weather broke, he'd get wet going back to Whitehall.

He turned back into the room, studying it expertly. The camera was set into the ventilation grid behind him, he knew. Then there'd be a microphone in the light socket. And another concealed in the over-large locking mechanism on the door. And it would be easy to have inserted another monitor in the edging around the table at which they would sit. Cuthbertson would have had it done, he guessed. The man liked electronic gadgetry.

Welcome the invention of the tape recorder, mused Charlie, his interest waning. He could still remember the days of silent note-takers and the irritable disagreements after a six-hour debriefing between operatives trying to remember precisely what had been said.

He heard footsteps and turned to the door expectantly, looking forward to the meeting with the Russian.

He liked Alexei Berenkov, he decided.

The Russian entered smiling, a shambling man with a bulging stomach, a tumble of coal-black hair and ready-to-laugh eyes set in a florid, over-indulged face. The cover of a wine importer, which had allowed frequent trips abroad, was well chosen, thought Charlie. Berenkov had had his own private wine bin at the Ritz and Claridge's and a permanent box at Ascot.

"Charlie!" greeted the Russian, expansively. He spread his arms and moved forward. Muffin made to shake hands, but Berenkov swept on, enveloping him in a hug. It wasn't a sham, remembered Charlie. They'd kept the man under observation for six months, before even beginning the concentrated investigation. Berenkov was a naturally exuberant extrovert, using the very attention he constantly attracted as a shield behind which to hide. Charlie stood with the man's arms around him, feeling foolish.

Thank God Snare and Harrison weren't there.

"It's good to see you, Alexei," he said, disentangling himself. He looked beyond, to the warder who stood uncertainly inside the door, frowning at the greeting.

"You can go," dismissed Charlie. Cuthbertson had arranged the meeting with his child-like interpretation of psychology and insisted just the two of them be in the room.

"I'm quite safe," Berenkov told the official. He thought the assurance amusing and shouted with laughter, slapping Charlie's shoulder. The warder hesitated, uncertainly. After several minutes, he shuffled away, flat-footedly. He'd stay very close, guessed Charlie. Cuthbertson would insist on a report from the man, despite all the recording apparatus.

"The only thing missing is some wine," apologized the Russian, playing the host. "It's a pity. This year I'd selected some really sensational Aloxe Corton."

Charlie smiled back, enjoying the performance.

"So they've sent you to find out what you can, thinking I'll be off-guard after the trial. And probably shocked by the sentence," attacked the Russian, suddenly. The smile had gone, like a light being extinguished.

Charlie shrugged, sitting in one of the padded chairs by the table. Berenkov was very clever, he decided.

"I'm sorry," said Charlie, in genuine embarrassment.

"I know it's bloody ridiculous. But they wouldn't listen."

Berenkov moved to the table, glancing up at the heavy light fitting.

"Probably," agreed Charlie, following Berenkov's look and recalling his earlier thought. "It's the most obvious place."

"Who are they, these fools who employ you?" demanded Berenkov.

Charlie settled comfortably. This was going to be enjoyable, he decided.

"It's no good, Alexei," he said, wanting to prolong it. "I made the point, saying you were obviously a professional who wouldn't break, even now. But they insisted. I've said I'm sorry."

Berenkov puffed his cheeks, indignantly. Aware every remark was being relayed, he rose to the meeting, like the actor he was.

"They're cunts," he said, offended. "I'm a loyal Russian."

"I know," agreed Charlie, sincerely. "But it was easier to come than to argue that you wouldn't give anything away about your system . . ."

He smiled, genuinely. "Anyway," he added, "I wanted to see you again."

It was an odd relationship between them, reflected Charlie. It was basically deep admiration from one professional to another, he supposed. Berenkov had realised, months before his arrest, that he was under observation. Charlie had made it obvious, in the end, hoping to frighten the man into an ill-considered move. Berenkov hadn't made one, of course. Instead, the knowledge had piqued his conceit and it had become a battle between them, an exercise in wits, like a game of postal chess. And Charlie had won, proving he was slightly the better of the two. So, added to Berenkov's admiration was an attitude of respect.

"Why weren't you at the trial?" Berenkov asked, settling at the table and taking, uninvited, one of Charlie's cigarettes.

"It was decided it was too dangerous," said Charlie,

unconvincingly repeating Cuthbertson's explanation. "We didn't want to risk identification. Your people would have photographed everyone going into the Old Bailey, wouldn't they?"

Berenkov frowned for a moment, then smiled at Charlie's head, looking up at the light.

"Oh yes," he agreed. "Every picture will be in Moscow by now."

That would put the fear of Christ up the Special Branch and Cuthbertson, Charlie knew. They'd had four men of their own photographing everyone within a quarter of a mile vicinity during the week-long trial. It would take them months to identify every face; but Cuthbertson would insist upon it—"mountains are just pieces of dust, all gathered together" was a new catch phrase from the department controller. Now he'd be shit scared there was the risk of his own men being identified.

"So Snare and Harrison got all the credit," jabbed Berenkov.

The Russian *was* bloody good, thought Charlie. It was not surprising he'd held the rank of General in the K.G.B. for the twenty years he'd operated in the West. His capture would be an enormous blow to Russia: perhaps even greater than they had realised.

"Something like that," agreed Charlie.

"They're no good," dismissed the prisoner. "Too smart . . . too keen to shine and impress people. Their performance in court was more like Sunday Night at the London Palladium. Send them on a field operation and we'd use it as a training exercise."

Oh God, how I'd like to be with Cuthbertson when the tapes are played back, thought Charlie. Please God let Snare and Harrison be there.

The Briton thought again of the life style that Berenkov had followed until his arrest six months earlier: despite the apparent *bonhomie,* the man must be suffering, he decided.

"What's it like here?" asked Charlie, curiously, gesturing to the prison around them.

"Known worse," replied Berenkov, lightly.

And he would have done, Charlie knew. The Russian admitted to being fifty, but Charlie assessed him ten years older. He'd have served in the Russian army during the war, probably as a field officer on the German Front. Certainly it was from Germany that he had appeared, posing as a refugee displaced by the division of his country, to enter Britain.

"But forty years!" reminded Charlie.

Berenkov stared at him, frowning, imagining for a moment that the Briton was serious. He shrugged, agreeing to whatever Charlie wanted to achieve.

"Don't be stupid," he answered. "I won't serve forty years and we all know it. I guess two, but it might be shorter: I'm very highly regarded in the Soviet Union. They'll arrange an exchange. All they need is a body."

And they almost had one four months ago at Checkpoint Charlie, remembered the Briton.

The K.G.B. general leaned back, reflectively.

"I tried to outwit you, Charlie. You know I did," he began, unexpectedly. "But more to cover up my network than for myself."

He was being truthful now, realised Charlie, the recording apparatus disregarded.

"You know what my feelings were, realising you were after me?" Berenkov stared across the table, intently.

"What?" prompted Charlie.

"Relief," answered Berenkov, simply. He leaned forward, arms on the table, gazing straight at the other man.

"You know what I mean, Charlie," he said, urgently. "Look at us. Apart from being born in different countries and being absolutely committed to opposite sides, we're practically identical. And we're freaks, Charlie. Whoever heard of two spies, both out in the field, alive and nudging fifty?"

Charlie shrugged, uncomfortably.

"I know," he agreed.

"I was losing my grip, Charlie," admitted Berenkov.

"And I think Moscow was beginning to realise it. I've been scared for the last two years. But now everything is all right."

"Sure?" questioned Charlie.

"Positive," insisted Berenkov, with his usual confidence. "Look at the facts, I'll spend a couple of years here, warm, safe and comfortable as a guest of Her Majesty's Government, then be exchanged ..."

He leaned back, eyes distant, reflecting his future.

"I've retired, Charlie," he said. "Waiting for me in Moscow is a wife I've only ever seen for two or three weeks a year, on phoney wine-buying trips to Europe. And a son of eighteen I've met just once ..."

He came back to the Briton.

"... he's studying engineering at Moscow University," continued Berenkov. "He'll pass with a First. I'm very proud."

Charlie nodded, knowing it would be wrong to interrupt the reminiscence.

"I shall go back to full honours fêted as a hero. I've a government apartment I've never seen and a dacha in the hills outside Moscow. I'll teach at the spy college and spend the summers in the sun at Sochi. Think of it, Charlie—won't it be wonderful!"

"Wonderful," said Charlie.

The Russian hesitated, appearing uncertain. The need to hit back at someone who had proved himself superior surfaced.

"What about you, Charlie?" worried the Russian. "What's your future ... where's your sunshine ... ?"

Outside, the rain finally broke, driven against the windows with sharp, hissing sounds by the growing wind. Charlie moved his foot inside the worn-out shoe. Bugger it, he thought.

"If I hadn't been caught, Charlie, I'd have been withdrawn. Operatives our age are expendable."

The memory of the exploding Volkswagen and the way it had ignited the body of Günther Bayer pushed itself into Charlie's mind.

"I know," he said, softly.

"But there is a difference," said Berenkov, scoring still. "Russia never forgets a spy . . . my release is guaranteed . . ."

He paused, allowing the point to register.

". . . but Britain couldn't give a bugger," he sneered. "I'd hate to work in your service, Charlie."

The man was right, accepted the Briton. The eagerness of the British Government to dissociate itself from a captured operative had always been obscene. How much enjoyment Cuthbertson and Wilberforce would get, cutting him off, thought Charlie, bitterly.

"It's a great incentive not to get caught," said Charlie, hollowly.

"Bullshit," replied Berenkov quickly. "How your people can ever expect anyone to work for them I'll never understand. Russia might have its faults . . . and it's got them, millions of them. But at least it's got loyalty."

"Moscow will be very strange to you, after so long," Charlie tried to recover.

Berenkov shrugged, uncaring.

"But I'll be able to wake up in the morning without those sixty seconds of gut-churning fear while you wait to see if you're alone . . . without having to turn immediately, to ensure that the pistol is still under the pillow and hasn't been taken by the man you always expect to be waiting at the end of the bed."

It was as if the other man were dictating the fears that he was daily experiencing, thought Charlie.

"How many more jobs will there be, Charlie?" pressed the Russian. "Will we get you next time? Or will you be lucky and survive a little longer?"

Charlie sighed, unable to answer.

"Perhaps I'll get a Whitehall desk and a travel organiser's job."

Berenkov shook his head.

"That's not the way your people work, Charlie," he replied, correctly. "You'll be for the dump."

Cuthbertson *had* been prepared to sacrifice him, Charlie knew. Ordering the three of them to return from East Berlin separately, then leaking the number of the Volkswagen that would be crossing last, had been a brilliant manoeuvre, guaranteeing that two operatives crossed ahead of it with the complete list of all Berenkov's East European contacts to make the Old Bailey prosecution foolproof.

It had just meant the demise of Charlie Muffin, that's all. Expendable, like Berenkov said.

"Worried about your network?" tried Charlie.

Berenkov smiled. "Of course not."

"So it hasn't been closed down," snatched Charlie.

Berenkov's smile faltered.

"How would I know?" he said. "I've been in custody for seven months already."

"We managed to get five," revealed Charlie.

The expression barely reached Berenkov's face. So there was more, discerned Charlie.

"Well, they had a good run and made some money," dismissed the Russian lightly. "And I always let them have their wine wholesale."

Charlie wondered the price of Aloxe Corton. It would be nice to take a bottle to Janet's flat. He had £5 and might be able to get some expenses from Cuthbertson. Then again, he contradicted, he might not. Accounts claimed he was £60 overdrawn and Cuthbertson had sent him two memoranda about getting the debt cleared before the end of the financial year. Bloody clerk.

"Will you come to see me?" asked the Russian. Quickly he added: "Socially, I mean."

"I'll try," promised Charlie.

"I'd appreciate it," replied Berenkov, honestly. "They have given me a job in the library, so I'll have books. But I'll need conversation."

The Russian *would* suffer, thought Charlie, looking around the prison room: the whole place had the institutionalised smell of dust, urine and paraffin heaters. It was a frightening contrast to the life he had known for so long. Charlie heard the scuff of the hovering warder outside the door. It had been a useful meeting, he decided. He wondered if Cuthbertson would realise it.

He rose, stretching.

"I really will try," he undertook.

Again there was the bear-hug of departure: the man still retained the odour of expensive cologne.

"Remember what I said, Charlie," warned Berenkov. "Be careful."

"Sure," agreed Charlie, easily.

Berenkov held him, refusing to let him turn away.

"I mean it, Charlie . . ."

He dropped his restraining hands, almost embarrassed.

". . . You've got a feel about you, Charlie . . . the feel of a loser . . ."

General Valery Kalenin was a short, square-bodied Georgian who regarded Alexei Berenkov as the best friend he had ever known, and recognised with complete honesty that the reason for this was that the other man had spent so much time away from Russia that it had been impossible for him to tire of the association, like everyone else did.

General Kalenin was a man with a brilliant, calculating mind and absolutely no social ability, which he accepted, like a person aware of bad breath or offensive perspiration. Because of a psychological quirk, which had long ceased bothering him, he had no sexual inclination, either male or female. The lack of interest was immediately detected by women, who resented it, and by men, who usually misinterpreted it, and were offended by what they regarded as hostile coldness, verging on contempt for their shortcomings compared to his intellect.

With virtually nothing to distract him apart from his absorption in the history of tank warfare, in which he was an acknowledged expert, Kalenin's entire existence was devoted to the *Komitet Gosudarstvennoy Bezopasnosti* and he had become a revered figure in the

K.G.B. of which he was now chief tactician and planner.

Utterly dedicated, he worked sixteen hours a day in Dzerzhinsky Square or in any of the capitals of the Warsaw Pact, of which he was over-all intelligence commander. Any surplus time was spent organising solitary war games with his toy tanks on the kitchen floor of his apartment in Kutuzovsky Prospekt. Only during the war games did General Kalenin feel his loneliness and regret his inability to make friends: it was always difficult to perform as the leader of both sides, even though he was scrupulously fair, never cheating with the dice.

The arrest of Berenkov had affected him deeply, although it would have been impossible for anyone to have realised it from his composure in the small conference chamber in the Kremlin complex.

"Berenkov *must* be exchanged," said the committee chairman, Boris Kastanazy, breaking into the General's reflections.

Kalenin looked warily at the man who formed the link between the Praesidium and the K.G.B. It was the fourth occasion he'd uttered the same sentence. Kalenin wondered if he were completely secure or whether he should be worried by this man.

"I know," responded Kalenin. There was no trace of irritation in his voice.

"And will be," he added. He wasn't frightened, he decided. And Kastanazy knew it. The man would be annoyed. He enjoyed scaring people.

"Not if the attempt to ensnare a British operative is handled with the stupidity surrounding the East Berlin border crossing."

"The officers who reacted prematurely have been reprimanded," reminded Kalenin.

Kastanazy moved, irritably.

"That's a stupid gesture; it wasn't the right man, so what does it matter? The important thing is that one of the best operatives the service ever had is rotting in a filthy jail and we're doing nothing about it."

Kastanazy was a pinch-faced, expressionless man who wore spectacles with which he fidgeted constantly, the way some men use worry beads.

"At the last full session of the Praesidium," said the chairman, slowly, gazing down at the revolving spectacles, "a lengthy discussion was held on the matter."

"I am aware how this committee was formed," said Kalenin. He would not be intimidated by the man, he decided.

"But I don't get the impression, Comrade General, that you fully appreciate the determination to retrieve General Berenkov."

"I assure you, Comrade Chairman," retorted the tiny K.G.B. chief, "that I do."

"Have plans been made?"

"I am in the course of formulating proposals," Kalenin tried to avoid.

"You mean you've done nothing?" demanded Kastanazy, sharply.

"I mean I do not intend embarking on anything that will worsen, rather than improve, the position of General Berenkov."

Kastanazy sighed, noisily, staring directly at the other man. When he spoke, he did so with care, wanting the words to register. He talked directly to the secretary sitting alongside, ensuring everything was correctly recorded for later submission to the Praesidium.

"I want you to leave the meeting understanding one thing . . ."

He paused, but Kalenin refused to prompt him, knowing it would show nervousness.

"I want you to fully appreciate," said Kastanazy, "that if General Berenkov isn't being received with full honours at Sheremetyevo airport resonably soon, the most stringent enquiry will be held . . ."

He hesitated again and Kalenin knew he had not finished.

". . . an enquiry, Comrade General, in which you will be the central character . . ."

3

Charlie Muffin wedged the saturated suede boots beneath the radiator, then spread his socks over the metal ribs to dry. There was a faint hissing sound.

The bottoms of his trousers, where the raincoat had ended, were concertinaed and sodden and he felt cold, knowing his shirt was wet where the coat had leaked. It was the newer of the two suits he possessed and now it would have to be dry-cleaned. It wouldn't be long before it started getting shiny at the seat, he thought, miserably.

Charlie wondered if he would catch influenza or a cold from his soaking; it would provide an excuse to stay away from the office for a few days. He stopped at the hope. The last time he'd had such a thought he had been a fifth grader, trying to avoid an English examination at Manchester Grammar School.

"Steady, Charlie," he advised himself. "Things aren't that bad."

He would have kept drier, he reflected, had he caught a taxi back from Wormwood Scrubs, instead of travelling by bus and underground from Shepherd's Bush. The sacrifice had been worth it, he decided. It meant an expenses profit of £2 and a bottle of wine for tonight.

"Aloxe Corton," he reminded himself. "Mustn't forget the name."

The dye had come out of his boots, staining his heels and between his toes a khaki colour. Barefoot, he padded into the lavatory opposite his office, from which he could always hear the flush and usually the

24

reason for it, filled a water glass with hot water and returned towards his office, pausing at the door. He'd only occupied it for three months, since Cuthbertson had decreed that the room adjoining his own suite and in which Charlie had worked during home periods for the past twenty years was big enough for two men. So Snare and Harrison had got the airy, oak-panelled room with its view of the Cenotaph. And Charlie—"as a senior operative, you'll have to be alone, old boy"—had been relegated to what had once been the secretaries' rest room, overlooking an inner courtyard where the canteen trash cans were kept. On the wall by the window there was still a white outline where the sanitary-towel dispenser had been: Janet had identified the mark and Charlie refused to have it painted over, knowing it offended Cuthbertson.

He entered the cramped room, sitting carefully at the desk, which was wedged tight against one wall. The wet trousers clung to his ankles and he grimaced, unhappily. Even with two men in it, he remembered, his old office was still bigger than that he was now forced to occupy. And it had had an electric fire, too, where he could have dried his trousers.

He stripped some blotting paper, soaked it in the glass and began sponging his feet, reflecting on his meeting with Berenkov. Had the Russian meant to tell him so much? he wondered. It could hardly have been a mistake; he wasn't the sort of man to allow errors. He'd been caught, contradicted Charlie. *That* had been a mistake. Or had it? Had Berenkov been incredibly clever, accepting his self-confessed fear and manoeuvred the whole thing, confident of repatriation as a hero after sentence?

He paused, left ankle across his right knee. Were his feelings for Berenkov admiration or envy? he wondered, suddenly.

"Good God!"

Snare stood at the doorway, gazing down at him.

"What the hell do you think you are doing?" demanded the younger man.

"Washing my feet," retorted Charlie, obviously. Snare's expressions of horror were encompassing the entire religious gamut, Charlie thought. He was embarrassed at being caught by the other man.

Snare leaned on the doorpost, knowing the discomfort and enjoying it.

"Very biblical," mocked Snare. "Can you do miracles, too?"

"Yes," said Charlie irritably. "I can come back from the dead out of burning Volkswagens."

The smile left Snare's face and he moved away from the doorway. The bastard *had* known, Charlie decided, even before they'd gone into East Berlin.

"The Director wants to see you," said Snare. Quickly he added, wanting to score, "With your shoes on."

"Then he'll have to wait," said Charlie. A faint mist was rising from his drying socks and shoes. And there was a smell, realised Charlie, uncomfortably.

"Shall I tell him ten minutes?"

"Tell him what you like," said Charlie. "I'm waiting for my socks to dry."

He was ready in fifteen minutes, but was delayed another ten by comparing two sheets in the Berenkov file.

"Charlie boy, you're a genius," he assured himself.

They were waiting for him, Charlie saw. Snare was standing at the window, appearing preoccupied with the view below. Harrison was sitting by the small table containing the newspapers and magazines, his back to the wall, determined to miss nothing. Wilberforce was in the leatherbacked lounging chair to the side of Cuthbertson's desk, disembowelling a pipe he never seemed to light, with a set of attachments that retracted into a single gold case. The second-in-command was a slightly built but very tall, fine-featured man with fingers so long they appeared to have an extra joint and of which he was overconscious, frequently making washing movements, covering one with the other, which drew attention to their oddness. He invariably wore gloves, even in the summer, and had a predilection for pastel-shaded shirts that he always wore with matching socks. Probably dryer than mine, thought Charlie, who still felt damp. He decided Wilberforce carried the pipe as a symbol of masculinity.

"More comfortable now?" greeted Cuthbertson, heavily.

The new Director was a very large but precise man, with a face permanently reddened by a sub-lieutenant's liking for curry at the beginning of his career in Calcutta, and a later tendency to blood pressure on the British General Staff. He had a distressingly phlegmy voice, which meant he bubbled rather than spoke words. Charlie found this offensive. But then he found most things about Cuthbertson offensive. The man's family was probably traceable back to Elizabethan times and there had been generals in it for three hundred years. It was with that rank, plus a D.S.O. and the inherited baronetcy originally conferred by George III, that Cuthbertson had left the Chief of Staff to head the department. His outlook and demeanour were as regimented as his brigade or Eton tie, the family-crested signet ring and the daily lunch at Boodle's. Which was precisely why he had been appointed, a government experiment to improve by strict discipline and army-type order a department that had suffered two humiliating—and worse, public—mistakes in attempting to establish systems in Poland and Czechoslovakia.

Charlie wondered how long it would take before they suffered their biggest mistake to date: not long, he decided, confidently.

"Much more comfortable, thank you, sir," replied Charlie. The term of respect sounded offensive. No one offered him a chair, so he stood casually at ease. On a parade ground, he thought, Cuthbertson would have put him on a charge.

"Which is more than I can say for myself," said Cuthbertson, softly. It was an affectation never to be seen to lose his temper, so it was impossible to gauge any mood from the gurgling tone in which the man spoke.

"Sir?"

"It has been my misfortune . . ."

He paused, gesturing to the others in the room.

". . . and the misfortune and embarrassment of my colleagues, to have listened to a tape recording that many people might construe as being almost treasonable . . ."

He stopped again, as if expecting Charlie to speak, but the man remained silent, eyes fixed on the Director's forehead. If he wriggled his toes, Charlie discovered, he could make a tiny squelching sound with his left boot.

"Psychologically," continued Cuthbertson, "today was the ideal time to interrogate Berenkov . . . bewildered and frightened by the severity of his sentence, cut off from life and eager to exchange every confidence with someone conducting an examination in a proper, sympathetic way . . ."

Charlie wondered at the text-book from which Cuthbertson would have read that thesis. It was probably a do-it-yourself paperback from W. H. Smith's, he decided. Snare turned away from the window, wanting to see Charlie suffer.

"Instead," continued the former army officer, "we got the meanderings of two men play-acting for the benefit of the recorders . . . recorders that Berenkov could only have learned about from you . . ."

It would have been a severe exercise of will to maintain the monotone, thought Charlie. He wondered why the man never cleared his throat. A nerve in Cuthbertson's left eyelid began twitching, indicating his anger. The man felt on his desk for a transcript.

". . . The Russian made a remark about age," said Cuthbertson, apparently reading. He'd rehearsed this part, Charlie realised.

The Director stood up, trying to hold Charlie's eyes.

"For you, it was a prophecy," declared Cuthbertson. "I've already sent to the Minister a copy of the transcript and my appreciation of it, together with my recommendation of your immediate premature departure from any position of authority in this department ... I don't want traitors working with me, Muffin."

Snare and Harrison were smirking, Charlie saw.

Silence settled like frost in the room. Charlie stayed unmoving, wanting Cuthbertson to finish completely, with no opportunity for retreat. What idiots they all were, he thought.

"Have you anything to say?" demanded Wilberforce, still rummaging into the bowl of his pipe. He would find it impossible to confront directly anyone being disciplined, Charlie realised. The permanent civil servant had waited a long time for this scene, Charlie knew. Why, he wondered, did Wilberforce hate him so?

"Does that mean I'm fired?" he asked, hopefully. He purposely omitted the "sir."

"It does not," said Cuthbertson. "I want you under constant supervision, where I can ensure you don't forget the terms of the Official Secrets Act by which you're bound for a lifetime but which, judging from this morning's performance, you have forgotten."

"Demotion?" asked Charlie.

"As far down as I can possibly achieve," confirmed Cuthbertson.

"So my allowance and salary will be cut?"

Cuthbertson nodded.

"And you've suggested all this in the letter to the Minister?" demanded Charlie. He was enjoying himself, he realised.

"That's an impudent question," said Cuthbertson huffily. "But yes, I have."

"Oh dear," said Charlie. "That was a silly thing to have done."

The silence this time was far more oppressive than that of a few moments before where Cuthbertson had announced his decision on Charlie's future. Wilberforce had stopped working on his pipe, but remained staring fixedly at it, as if he expected to find a clue in the blackened bowl. Harrison shifted uncomfortably in the chair, as if he wanted to use a lavatory, and Snare looked hurriedly from person to person, seeking a clue from the others on what reaction to make. The lobes of Cuthbertson's ears flushed and the nerve in his eye increased its tic.

"Impudence will not gain the dismissal to get whatever redundancy pay you imagine is owed you," rejected Cuthbertson, haughtily.

For the first time, Charlie lowered his eyes from the man's forehead, staring directly at him. Cuthbertson appeared to realise Charlie was not scared and blinked, irritably. It was very rare for Cuthbertson to encounter somebody not in awe of him, Charlie guessed.

He'd made them suffer, he decided: he had very little to lose. Nothing, in fact. Their decision about Charlie Muffin had been made months ago. He supposed he should consider himself lucky he was still alive.

"There is a procedure," he began slowly. "Innovated by your predecessors . . . a procedure that the Minister likes followed because it has shown such success in the past . . ."

". . . but one which was overlooked in the Polish and Czechoslovakian disasters," tried Snare, eager to impress his mentor.

Charlie turned to him, frowning.

"I'm sorry?" he said, knowing the effect would be destroyed if the man were forced to repeat it.

"Nothing," said Snare. "Just a comment."

"Oh," said Charlie. He still waited, as if expecting Snare to repeat himself. Wince, you bastard, he thought. At last he looked back to Cuthbertson.

"I'm sure it will be followed in the case of my interview with Berenkov," he continued. "Once established, procedures are rigidly followed. And *you've* decreed that, of course."

Cuthbertson nodded, cautiously. The left eye twitched and Charlie thought he detected Wilberforce looking surreptitiously at him.

"What are you talking about?" demanded the Director.

He was beginning to become unsettled, Charlie decided, happily, detecting the apprehension in that unpleasant voice.

"The detailed analysis," said Charlie. "By psychological experts, not only of the tapes but of the film that was shot in the interview room."

"What about it?"

"Your reaction to the meeting and your recommendation was made without waiting for the results of that analysis?"

"There was no need to wait," defended Cuthbertson.

"As I said," reminded Charlie. "A silly thing to have done."

They were all frightened, he knew, without being able to appreciate their mistake. It was time to change his approach, he determined.

"My meeting with Berenkov was one of the most productive I can remember having had with a captured spy," asserted Charlie, brutally. "And the analyst's department will confirm it . . ."

He paused, deciding to allow himself the conceit.

". . . they always have in the past," he added.

Wilberforce was back at his pipe but the other three were staring at him, unmoving.

"Close examination of the transcript," continued Charlie, hesitating for another aside, ". . . much closer than you've allowed yourselves . . . will confirm several things. Berenkov admitted his nerve had gone. If he knew it, then Moscow certainly did. And the Kremlin would have acted upon that knowledge. A replacement would have been installed in London, long before we got on to Berenkov. He's important, certainly. But because of what he'd done in the past, not for what he might have done in the future. We haven't broken the Russians' European spy system. I estimate his successor will have been here for a year, at least . . . so you've got to begin all over again . . ."

The vibration in Cuthbertson's eye was now so severe he put his hand up to cover it.

"There are a number of his existing network whom we haven't caught, either," enlarged Charlie. "Consider the film and watch the facial reactions when I announced, quite purposely, that we have caught five. Slow the film: it will show a second's look of triumph, indicating there are some still free . . ."

Charlie stopped again, swallowing. They were so innocent, he thought, looking at the four men. Wilberforce was like them, he decided, institutionalised by training according to a rule book and completely unaware of what they should be doing.

". . . And he told us how to find them," Charlie threw out.

He waited. They would have to crawl, he determined.

"How?" asked Cuthbertson, at last.

"By boasting," explained Charlie. "Letting them have their wine wholesale wasn't a smart, throw-away remark. It was exactly the grandiose sort of thing that an extrovert like Berenkov would have done. And he would have kept scrupulous records: a spy always complies with every civil law of any country in which he's operating. Check every wholesale outlet against income tax returns and you'll find the rest of the network. The five we've got are all on it—I checked while my socks were drying."

He looked carefully at each man, allowing his head to shake almost imperceptibly.

"I'm *really* sorry that the meeting was regarded by you all as such a failure," he insisted, straining for the final insult. "And I'm sure the Minister will be surprised when he considers your views against those of the detailed analysis. Now, if you'll excuse me, I'll clear my desk . . ."

He drew almost to attention, coming back to Cuthbertson.

"Have I your permission to leave, sir?"

The Director seemed intent on the papers lying before him and it was several minutes before he spoke.

"We could have been a little premature in our assessment," he conceded. The words were very difficult for him, Charlie knew. He noted the pronoun: within the day, the mistake would be shown not to be Cuthbertson's but someone else wrongly guiding him.

Charlie said nothing, knowing that silence was his best weapon now.

"Perhaps," continued the Director, "we should reexamine the tape and discuss it tomorrow."

"Re-examine the tape by all means," agreed Charlie, deciding to abandon the "sir": Cuthbertson didn't deserve any respect. "I'm sure the Minister will expect a more detailed knowledge of it at the meeting you will inevitably have," he added. "But tomorrow I'm going on leave . . . you've already approved it, you'll remember?"

"Of course," said Cuthbertson, groping on the desk again, as if seeking the memorandum of agreement.

"So perhaps we'll discuss my future in a fortnight?"

Cuthbertson nodded, half concurring, half dismissing. His presence embarrassed them, Charlie knew. They would welcome the two-week gap more than he.

"I can go?" pressed Charlie.

"Yes," said Cuthbertson, shortly.

Outside the office, Charlie turned right, away from his own room, feeling very happy. Janet was sitting expectantly at her desk, solemn-faced.

"I've been dumped," announced Charlie.

"I know," said Cuthbertson's secretary. "I typed the report to the Minister. Oh Charlie, I'm so sorry."

"So are they," said Charlie, brightly. "They've made a balls of it. Tonight still okay?"

The girl stared at him, uncertainly.

"Does it mean you won't be demoted to some sort of clerk?"

"Don't know," said Charlie. "Seven o'clock?"

She nodded, bewildered.

Whistling tunelessly, Charlie wandered back to his

cramped room. The affair with Janet had only begun
four weeks ago and still had the excitement of newness
about it. Pity the holiday would intrude: but that was
important. Edith needed a vacation, he decided, thinking fondly of his wife.

And so did he, though for different reasons.

General Kalenin pushed aside the file containing the
questionable plans for Berenkov's release, lounging
back in his chair to look over the Kremlin complex.
Most of the office lights were out, he saw. How different it had been in Stalin's time, he remembered, when
people remained both day and night at their desks,
afraid of a summons from the megalomaniac insom-
niac.

He looked back to the unsatisfactory dossier. He
was more apprehensive now than he had ever been
then, he decided. The Berenkov affair could topple
him, Kalenin realised. It wasn't the purge and disgrace
that frightened him. It was being physically removed
from the office in the Lubyanka buildings in Dzerzhinsky Square. Without a job, he would have nothing, he
thought. He'd commit suicide, he decided, quite ration-
ally. It wasn't the first time he'd thought of such a
thing and there was no fear in the consideration. A
revolver, he determined. Very quick. And befitting an
officer.

He sighed, hearing midnight strike. Slowly he
packed the papers into his personal safe, trying to
arouse some anticipation for the war game he had
prepared when he got to his apartment.

Tonight he was going to start the Battle of Kursk,
the greatest tank engagement in history. But his mind
wouldn't be on it, he knew.

4

Charlie had seen advertised in the *New Yorker* the orange Gucci lounging pyjamas, with the matching rhinestone-encrusted sandals in which Janet greeted him.

She smelt fresh and expensive and when he kissed her, just inside the doorway of the Cadogan Square flat, he could feel she was still warm from her bath. It was nice of her to go to all the trouble, thought Charlie.

"I've bought some wine," he announced.

She accepted the bag from him and extracted the bottle.

"Lovely," she said. "Spanish burgundy."

"They didn't have Aloxe Corton," he said. They had, but it had been priced at £4.

"What?" she said, moving further into the flat.

Janet was using him, he decided, as he entered the antique-adorned living-room behind her, watching her body beneath the silk. She had a lovely ass.

Had she been born in a council house instead of on a country estate and attended a state school instead of Roedean, Janet would have been a slut, Charlie decided. She had an amorality sometimes found in the rich that made her sexually promiscuous, experimental and constantly avaricious. Rich enough—first from an aunt's, then a cousin's inheritance—to do nothing. Janet worked for £4,000 a year as Cuthbertson's private secretary and never had any money. To get it, she had even whored, in a dilettante, friends-only way— "making a hobby pay for itself"—and enjoyed boasting about it, imagining Charlie would be impressed or excited by it. Charlie felt she was exactly his sort of woman. And in addition, very useful. And she really was very good at her hobby between those silk sheets that always slipped off the bed, so that his bum got cold.

Quite unoffended, Charlie knew he was another experiment, like working for Sir Henry Cuthbertson, who was her godfather, and drinking warm bitter, which she had done for the first time on their initial date in the dive bar of the Red Lion, near Old Scotland Yard, and declared it, politely, to be lovely. Charlie was "other people," a person to be studied like she had examined dissected frogs at her Zürich finishing school after leaving Sussex.

"Like the duchess screwing the dustman," he reflected, aloud, stretching his feet towards the electric fire. They were still damp, he saw, watching the steam rise.

She reappeared from the kitchen, corkscrew in hand. She was a tall girl, hair looped long to her shoulders, bordering a face that needed only a little accent around the deep brown, languorous eyes and an outline for the lips that were inclined to pout.

"What about a duchess?" she queried.

"You look like one," said Charlie, easily.

Who was using whom? he wondered, smiling up at her. Poor Janet.

He pulled the wine, filling the glasses she offered.

"Love or what you will," he toasted.

She drank, swallowing heavily.

"Very nice," she said bravely.

They had bred good manners in Switzerland, thought Charlie. He smiled, imagining Berenkov's reaction to the wine. It was bloody awful.

"For a man who has been demoted, you're remarkably unconcerned," said Janet, sitting opposite. She wasn't wearing a bra, he realised.

"I told you, they've made a balls," he said. Rough talk would fit the image she wanted, he decided. He refilled his glass, ignoring her: it was unfair to expect her to drink it.

"How?"

"Completely misread the interview," he reported. "They have determined to get rid of me, certainly. But it won't work this time."

"Cuthbertson won't apologise," predicted Janet.

The fact that she was his god-daughter was incredibly useful, reflected Charlie: no one in the department knew the man like she did.

"He'll have to."

She shook her head.

"I know Sir Henry. He's a bastard."

"So am I," responded Charlie. "Funny thing is, nobody has realised it. It'll be the ruin of them."

She smiled at the boast. It was a normal reaction, she supposed. His pride must be badly bruised: he'd once been the most important operative in the department.

"I've cooked a meal, so we can eat here," she announced, wanting to move him away from the afternoon.

And not run the risk of being seen by any of your friends, thought Charlie. She would be very embarrassed by him, he knew. He was very happy with the proposal: there was no outing they would mutually enjoy and whatever they tried would have cost money and he didn't have any. And she would never think of paying.

"What happened after I left?" asked Charlie, spreading the salmon mousse on the toast.

The girl sighed. The preoccupation was to be expected, she thought, but it made him boring.

"They went potty," said Janet. "Wilberforce was sent to retrieve the report to the Minister, but it had already gone. So Sir Henry dictated a contradicting amendment, then scrapped it because it seemed ridiculous. When I left, he was making arrangements to dine the Minister at Lockets to explain everything."

"And who got the blame?" queried Charlie.

"Wilberforce," answered Janet. "Poor man. Uncle treats him almost like a court jester."

"Masochist," identified Charlie. "Gets a sexual thrill out of being tongue-lashed."

She believed him, realised Charlie, seeing the interested look on her face. To correct the misunderstanding seemed too much bother.

He cut into the *steak au poivre,* sipping the wine she had provided.

"This is good," he complimented.

"Margaux," explained Janet, patiently. "Daddy takes the production of the vineyard. This is '62."

Charlie nodded, as if he'd recognised the vintage.

"Where did you learn to cook like this?"

"They thought it important at school."

"What have Snare and Harrison been told to do?" he probed, insistently. She obviously hadn't understood the wording of the Official Secrets Act she had promised to obey seven months earlier.

"Interrogate Berenkov again."

"Oh Christ," said Charlie, putting aside his knife and fork. "That's a tape I'd love to hear."

She pushed away her plate, fingering the stem of her wine glass.

"I'm very fond of you, Charlie," she announced, suddenly.

At least she didn't make any pretence of love, he thought. He hoped she wasn't moving to end the affair; he wasn't ready for it to end yet. He gazed across the table, admiring her. Certainly not yet.

He waited, apprehensively.

"What are you going to do? They're determined to get you out," she said.

Charlie stopped eating, appetite gone.

"I know," he said, completely serious. "And it frightens me to death. They won't let me go, because they want me under observation. Or stay, because they detest me. So I'm faced with working for the next fifteen years as a clerk."

"You couldn't stand that, Charlie."

"I've got no bloody choice, have I? I've devoted my life to the service. I love it. There's not another sodding thing I could do, even if they'd let me."

He *did* love the life, he decided, adding to both their glasses. Because he was so good at it.

It had been wonderful before Cuthbertson and the army mafia had arrived, when his ability had been properly recognised.

The Director had been Sir Archibald Willoughby, who'd led paratroopers into Arnhem with his batman carrying a £20 hamper from Fortnum & Mason, and Venetian goblets for the claret in special leather cases. He was cultivating Queen Elizabeth and Montana Star roses in Rye now, hating every moment of it. There'd been two written invitations to visit him since his summary retirement, but so far Charlie had avoided it. They'd drink too much whisky and become maudlin about previous operations, he knew. And there was no way they could have kept the conversation off Bill Elliot.

On the day of the purge, Elliot had been sent home early because Cuthberson, who read spy novels, imagined he would find evidence of a traitor if he turned out every desk and safe in the department.

Elliot had walked from the room without a word, gone directly to the hide at the bottom of the garden from which he had earned the reputation of being one of Britain's leading amateur ornithologists and blown the top of his head away with an army-issue Webley fired through the mouth. He had been crying and he'd made a muck of it, so it had taken two days for him to die.

The suicide had slotted neatly into Cuthbertson's "who's to blame" mentality, despite the wife's unashamed account to the police, and Elliot had been labelled responsible for the Warsaw and Prague débâcles. It would be nice, reflected Charlie, to prove Cuthbertson wrong about that. Like everything else.

"Sure they wouldn't let you retire, prematurely?" asked Janet, breaking Charlie's silent reminiscence.

"Positive," asserted Charlie. "And I don't think I'd want to. At least rotting as a clerk would mean a salary of some sort. I wouldn't live off a reduced pension."

"I thought Edith had money."

"She's loaded," confirmed Charlie. "But my wife is tighter than a seal's ass-hole."

She smiled, nodding. It really was the sort of language she expected, Charlie realised.

"Do you know there are receipted bills at home dating back ten years. And if you asked her the amount, she could remember," he added.

"Why not leave her?"

"What for?" challenged Charlie. "Would you have me move in here, a worn-out old bugger of forty-one without a bank account of his own who can only afford Spanish plonk."

She reached across, squeezing his hand.

"From the performance so far, you're hardly worn out," contradicted Janet. "But no, Charlie. I wouldn't."

"So I've got to stay, haven't I?—tethered to a job that doesn't want me. And at home, to a wife who's not very interested."

"Poor Charlie," she said. She didn't sound sad, he thought.

He gestured round the apartment, then nodded towards her.

"All this will end, when I'm transferred, won't it?"

"I expect so," she said, always honest, looking straight at him.

"Pity."

"It's been fun," she said. She made it sound like a skiing lesson or a day out at Ascot when she'd picked a winner.

"Shall we go to bed?" he suggested.

"That's what you came here for."

They took a long time with each other, exploring; like children in bicycle sheds at school, thought Charlie, biting at her thigh. Just more comfortable, that's all.

"Don't. That hurts."

"So does what you're doing. I can feel your teeth."

"Want me to stop?"

"No."

"Charlie."

"What?"

"Your feet are a funny brown colour."

"My shoes leaked. The dye won't come off."

"Poor Charlie."

Then:

"I like what you're doing, Charlie."

"Where did you learn to do *that?*" he said, with difficulty.

"At school."

All that and cooking too, reflected Charlie. He winced, conscious of her teeth again. He should have washed his feet a second time, he told himself. She'd bathed, after all.

Charlie and his wife crossed on the following night's ferry from Southampton, so they were in Cherbourg by 6:30 in the morning.

Charlie liked driving Edith's Porsche, enjoying the power of machinery performing fully in the manner for which it was designed. I perform best fully extended, he thought, looking sideways at the woman as they climbed the curling road out of the French port and thinking of the previous night. Had Janet been acting her whore's role when she'd cried, he wondered.

Edith was a handsome woman, decided Charlie, as she smiled back at him. She had wound the window down, so that her naturally blonde hair tangled in the wind. She was definitely very lovely, he thought, her face almost unlined and no sag to the skin around her throat. He was very lucky to have her as a wife.

They stopped at Caen to look around the war museum and still easily reached Paris by noon. While Edith sipped kir on the pavement outside Fouquet's, Charlie telephoned their lunch reservation.

They ate at the Tour d'Argent, fond of the view across the Quai de la Tournelle to the Notre Dame.

With the *filet de sole cardinale*, Charlie ordered Corton Charlemagne and then—"we're on holiday, after all"—a half bottle of Louis Roederer with the *soufflé vallesse*, which he later agreed was an ostentatious mistake.

"You enjoy spending money, don't you, Charlie?" she said, as they unpacked at the Métropole-Opéra.

"Do you begrudge it?" he asked, immediately.

"You know I don't," she said, quickly, frightened of offending him. "But I saw the bill. It was over £50."

"But worth it," he defended.

He sat watching her change, enjoying her body. She was very well preserved, he thought, admiringly. Her waist was bubbled only slightly over the panty girdle, which he didn't think she needed anyway, and her legs were firm and unveined. Her full breasts fell forward as she unclipped her bra and she became conscious of his attention, covering herself like a surprised schoolgirl.

"What are you looking at?"

"What do you think?"

"Don't," she protested, emptily, pleased at the attention. She loved him very much and it frightened her sometimes.

Janet liked him admiring her body, Charlie compared, even insisting they make love with the light on. Edith always wanted it dark. Women were funny, he thought: his wife had much the better body. She should learn to be proud of it, not shy.

Edith was a comfortable woman to be with, he decided, the sort you didn't have to talk to all the time. With Janet three minutes of silence was construed either as boredom or boring so there was always a frenzy of meaningless chatter, like annoying insects on a summer's picnic. He definitely preferred Edith, he decided. They were friends, more than lovers, he thought. But very much lovers; Edith had a remarkable appetite for a woman of forty.

She backed towards him, the zip of her dress undone.

"Do me up."

"Why don't we undo it?"

"There isn't time."

"For what?"

"Don't muck about, Charlie. Tonight."

He fastened the dress: she didn't bulge it anywhere, he saw.

He gave every indication of loving her, she thought, patting her hair into place before the dressing table.

"Promise me something, Charlie," she said, crossing the room to him and placing her hands upon his shoulders. She was very serious, he realised. Her eyes were quite wet.

"What?"

"You won't leave me because of this office business, will you?"

"You know I won't," chided Charlie. "I've told you not to worry."

"I can't help it," said Edith, who ten years earlier had occupied the position that Janet now held as secretary to Sir Archibald Willoughby. Charlie had told her in detail of his treatment since Cuthbertson's arrival.

He stood up, coming level with her.

"I *love* you, Edith," he insisted, putting his hands round her waist. "I promise you that everything will work out. They're bloody fools."

"They can't be as stupid as you think."

"You wouldn't believe it!"

He kissed her, very softly, and she clung to him, head deep into his shoulder.

"I'm so worried about you, Charlie."

He stroked her neck, lips against her hair.

"I'm a survivor, Edith. Don't forget that. I always have been."

She shook her head, dismissing the assurance.

"Not this time, Charlie."

"We'll see, darling. We'll see."

Edith had alotted £100 a day for their holiday and Charlie drove eastwards from Paris the following morning £10 under budget, which pleased her.

Financial security meant everything to Edith, he

knew, as it always had to her family. She couldn't temper her attitude, despite what had happened to her father. He had been a bank manager in Reigate, a
respected Freemason, church deacon and treasurer to
the local Rotary Club. And he'd embezzled £600 to
cover stupidly incurred gambling debts he was too
proud to ask his rich wife to settle, shocking her and
Edith by the knowledge that he feared their contempt
and attitude to money more than the ignominy of a jail
sentence.

Edith had never forgotten the barrier that money
had created between her parents and tried desperately
to avoid it arising between her and Charlie. She was
terrified that she was failing.

Charlie had planned the holiday with care, determined they should enjoy themselves. In Reims, they
stayed at La Paix but ate at Le Florence, on the Boule-
vard Foch, dining off *pâté de canard truffé* and *lan-
goustine au ratafia,* drinking the house-recommended
Mauereuil. The next day, Charlie drove hard, wanting
to reach the German border by the evening. They
stayed in Sarreguemines, where Charlie remembered
the *Rôtisserie Ducs de Lorraine* on Rue Chamborand
from an operation eight years earlier.

"The duck is as good as it ever was," he declared at
the table that night.

"I wish we could stay in France," said Edith, almost
to herself.

"I thought you were looking forward to seeing Austria and Germany in the autumn."

"I was," she agreed. "But not any more. Not now."

"What's wrong?" he asked.

"You do love me, don't you, Charlie?"

"Yes, Edith," he answered, holding her eyes.

"I know I'm inclined to keep a pretty close check on
money," she said, looking down into her wine glass and
embarking upon a familiar path. "But I can't help it:
it's bred into me. But I regard it as our money, Charlie. Not just mine. Spend all of it, if you want to."

He waited.

"I mean, it wouldn't matter if you were downgraded . . . we wouldn't starve or anything. And it would be safer, after all."

"I'll have Cuthbertson begging me for help," predicted Charlie. "And it'll be my money that supports us."

Why, thought the woman sadly, did he have to have that bloody grammar-school pride. Just like her damned father.

5

The priority coded warning had come from the C.I.A. Resident at the Moscow embassy in advance of the diplomatic bag containing the full report, so the Director was already alerted and waiting when the messenger arrived at Langley.

He spent an hour examining the messages, then analysing the station head's assessment, reading it alongside the report that had come in two days earlier from the agency monitoring station in Vienna, which had fed his excitement the moment the initial Moscow report had been received.

Finally he stood up, gazing out over the Virginia countryside, where the leaves were already rusting into autumn.

Garson Ruttgers was a diminutive, frail man who deliberately cultivated a clerk-like appearance with half-lens spectacles that always appeared about to fall off his nose and slightly shabby, Brooks Brothers suits, invariably worn with vests, and blue, button-down-collared shirts. He smoked forty cigarettes a day against doctor's advice, convincing himself he compensated by an almost total abstinence from liquor, and was consumed by the ambition to become to the C.I.A. what Hoover had been to the F.B.I.

In a period that included the last year of the Second World War—when he had been a major in the O.S.S.—and then in the Korean conflict, he had killed (by hand because weapons would have made a noise and attracted attention) ten men who had threatened his exposure as an agent. Never, even in moments of recollection, had he reproached himself about it, even though two of his victims had been Americans whose loyalty he only suspected but could not disprove, and so had disposed of just in case.

That more people had not been killed with the same detachment was only because he had spent nearly eighteen years in Washington and the need had not arisen. He was, Garson Ruttgers convinced himself, a complete professional. A psychiatrist, knowing of his tendency to kill without compunction, would have diagnosed him a psychopath.

Ruttgers shivered, suddenly frightened by the information that lay before him. There could only be one conclusion, he judged. And the British, whom he regarded as amateurs, were bound to screw it up.

He dispatched a "most urgent" classified instruction to the embassy, ordering the Resident back to Washington on the next civilian aircraft, guaranteeing the man's presence in the capital at dawn the following day by arranging for a military plane to be specially available at the first airfield in the west.

Building a margin for any flight problems, he arranged the meeting with the Secretary of State, Willard Keys, at noon, cautioning in their telephone conversation that Keys might want to request an immediate meeting with the President.

From the computer in the Langley headquarters Ruttgers had within two hours a complete print-out on the man named in the report lying on his desk. It was very brief, as Ruttgers had anticipated: a man like General Valery Kalenin used anonymity like a cloak, he knew. Annexed to the print-out was the brief confirmation: "no photograph known to exist."

It *had* to be right, assessed Ruttgers, summarily cancelling all appointments and meetings during the next week.

There had never been an opportunity like this, he reflected. If they could get involved, the Agency would wipe away all the post-Watergate criticism. Internal telephone tapping, the Bay of Pigs and the Rockefeller

Commission would be laughed at. And Garson Ruttgers would achieve the awe that had surrounded Hoover.

That night Ruttgers broke his habit and had two brandies after dinner; without them, he decided, he wouldn't be able to sleep. He looked upon the second drink as a celebration in advance.

William Braley's cover as C.I.A. Resident in Moscow was as cultural attaché to the U.S. embassy. He was a puffy-faced, anaemic-looking man with a glandular condition that put him twenty-eight pounds overweight, pebble glasses that made him squint and the tendency to asthma when under pressure. He arrived in Washington at 10 A.M., delayed by fog at Frankfurt, gravel-eyed through lack of sleep and wheezing from apprehension.

Ruttgers would be furious if it transpired he had overreacted, he knew, thrusting the inhaler into his mouth in the back of the Pontiac taking him and the Director into Washington.

The prospect of meeting the Secretary of State terrified him: he wouldn't be able to use the breathing aid at the meeting, he thought, worriedly. Keys might be offended. He was rumoured to have a phobia about health.

"It could be nothing," Braley cautioned Ruttgers, hopefully. If he expressed doubt in advance, perhaps the recriminations wouldn't be so bad.

Ruttgers shook his head, determined.

"No way, Bill," dismissed the Director, who took pride in his hunches and knew this had the feel of a defection. "You got it right the first time. I'm proud of you."

Keys was waiting for them in his office in the Executive Building, a taciturn, aloof man, whose careful enunciation, like a bored educationalist in a school for retarded children, concealed a word-stumbling shyness. He knew the shell of arrogance beneath which he concealed himself caused dislike, which exacerbated the speech defect when meeting strangers for the first time.

Ruttgers had submitted a full report overnight and it lay now, dishevelled, on the Secretary of State's desk.

"Don't you think we're assuming a lot?" asked Keys, seating them considerately in armchairs before the fire. Braley remained silent, taking his lead from his superior sitting opposite. The fat man seemed unwell, thought the Secretary, distastefully. He hoped it wasn't anything contagious.

"I don't think so, Mr. Secretary," argued Ruttgers. "Consider the facts and equate them against the computer information."

Keys waited, nodding encouragement. Ruttgers would think him obtuse, the Secretary knew, unhappily.

"Until last week," explained Ruttgers, "there wasn't a Western embassy in Moscow who had a clue what Kalenin looked like . . . no one even knew for sure that he existed. Then, without any apparent reason, he turns up at one of our own receptions, a party considered so unimportant that apart from our own ambassador, it was only attended by First Secretaries and freeloaders with nowhere else to go on a dull night."

He nodded sideways to Braley, aware of the man's apprehension and trying to relax him.

"Thank God Bill was there, able to realise the significance."

"And what was that?" asked Keys, seeking facts rather than impressions.

"A man known only by an incredible reputation attends an unimportant function," he repeated. "He stays for two hours and makes a point of speaking almost exclusively to the British military attaché . . ."

Ruttgers grew uncomfortable at Keys's complete lack of reaction.

". . . And if that isn't odd enough," the Director hurried on, desperately, "a man of whom no photographs are known to exist, willingly poses for his picture to be taken . . ."

"How do we know it *is* Kalenin," butted in Keys, "if there haven't been any pictures."

"*Known* pictures," qualified Ruttgers. "We've had photographs compared with every Praesidium group taken over the last twenty years. The one established fact about Kalenin is his incredible survival . . . he appears in official pictures dating back two decades . . ."

Ruttgers waved his own file, like a flag. ". . . examine it," he exhorted the Secretary. "Six photographs of the most secretive man in the Soviet Union . . ."

Keys sighed. On amorphous interpretations such as this, he thought, the policies of a nation could be changed. It was little wonder there were so many crises.

"All this," stressed Ruttgers, "just three days after one of the most vicious diatribes ever published in *Pravda* and by *Izvestia* about lack of State security . . . an attack that can only be construed as a direct criticism of Kalenin . . ."

Keys waved a hand, still unconvinced.

"What do you think, Mr. Braley?" he asked. He was not interested, but it would give him time to consider what he'd read in the file and consider it against Ruttgers's conviction.

"It's strange, sir," managed the fat man, breathily. "I know it appears vague. But I seriously interpret it as indicating that Kalenin is considering the idea of coming across. Which is what worries me . . ."

"Worries you . . . ?"

"Our reception was the only Western diplomatic function that week . . . Kalenin used us, just to reach the British. As soon as we realised who he was, I and the ambassador tried to get involved. The man was positively rude in rejecting us."

Keys pursed his lips, with growing acceptancy. On the other side of the desk, Ruttgers frowned, annoyed the Secretary wasn't showing the enthusiasm he had expected. He gestured towards the dossier.

"And don't forget the Viennese reports," he continued encouragingly. "In Prague, according to our Austrian monitor, *Rude Pravo* have actually named Kalenin. No newspaper in the East does that without specific Praesidium instructions . . . the man's being purged. There can't be any doubt about it. He knows it and wants to run."

"To the British?"

"That's how it looks."

"I'd like more information upon which to make a judgment," complained Keys, cautiously. He'd use the antiseptic spray in the office when the two had gone: Braley looked as if he could be consumptive.

"As far as Russia is concerned, sir," offered Braley, "the indications we've got so far and those which are in the last report, are amazingly informative."

"Have you tried the British?"

"Of course," said Braley. "Their attitude encourages our conviction."

Keys waited.

"They've gone completely silent," reported Braley. He paused, like Ruttgers expecting some reaction. When none came, he added: "For a closed community like Moscow, that's unheard of. We live so cut off from everything that embassy-to-embassy contact, particularly between ourselves and the British, is far greater than anywhere else. For the past five days, I've tried to encourage a meeting, on any level . . ."

"And?"

"The British Embassy is tighter than the Kremlin itself."

"It certainly looks unusual," conceded Keys, finally. "If Kalenin is thinking of coming over, for whatever reason, how close are we to the British for access?"

Ruttgers controlled the sigh of impatience. He wasn't waiting until the British had finished, he had decided. That could take years.

"That's what made me request this meeting," said the Director. "The British have just had a major overhaul, throwing out nearly everyone."

"So?"

"I don't think they could properly handle something this big. It'll go wrong."

"How important is Kalenin?" asked Keys.

Ruttgers hesitated. At last, he thought, the doubtful son of a bitch is coming round.

"I don't think," he replied, slowly, "that I can think of a Russian whose defection would be more important in the entire history of communism . . . except perhaps Stalin."

Keys sat back, bemused at the analysis. Ruttgers was absolutely convinced, he decided.

"But surely . . ." he started to protest.

". . . he's lived through it all," insisted Ruttgers. "Stalin . . . Beria . . . Khrushchev and Bulganin . . . Brezhnev . . . there is not one single Russian better able to tell us not only what happened in the past, but what might occur in the future. His value is incalculable."

Ruttgers *had* been right in seeking the meeting, decided Keys. He'd tell the President at the afternoon briefing.

"I agree," said the Secretary. "We've got to get involved."

Ruttgers smiled and Braley found his breathing easier.

"But be careful," added Keys. "If the shit hits the fan, I want us wearing clean white suits. Hand-shakes in space and *détente* are important at the moment."

"I know," assured Ruttgers. He paused, uncertain about the commitment at the final moment of making it. The risks were enormous. But then so was the chance of glory.

"I thought I'd do it personally," he announced.

Keys stared at the C.I.A. chief, the words jamming in the back of his throat.

"Do you think that's wise?" he queried, finally.

"It's got to be someone of authority . . . someone who can make decisions on the spot," argued Ruttgers.

Keys looked down at the photographs of Kalenin

smiling up at him from the desk. Such an ordinary little man, he thought. Was he really worth it?

"I think it's very dangerous," judged Keys.

"So do I," agreed Ruttgers. "But I think the potential rewards justify it."

Keys nodded slowly, indicating Braley.

"I think you should be seconded to it, as well," he said. "You've encountered Kalenin, after all. And if the need to go into Moscow arrives, your visa is valid."

Braley smiled and felt his lungs tighten again.

The Secretary of State turned back to the Director.

"Keep me completely informed . . . at all times," he instructed. "I don't like it . . . I don't like it at all."

Kalenin crouched on the kitchen floor of his apartment, frowning at the tank displacement before him. He'd been fighting the Battle of Kursk for over a week now and it wasn't going at all well. Unless there was a sudden change of luck, the Germans were going to reverse historical fact and win. He stood up, bored with the game.

What, he wondered, would be his worth to the West? It was important to calculate the amount to reflect his value, without being ridiculous. He smiled, happy at the thought. Five hundred thousand dollars, he decided. Yes—that was just about right.

The Customs inspector at Southampton located the second litre of brandy in Charlie's overnight case and sighed, irritably. Why was there always a bloody fool? He held up the bottle, not bothering with the question.

"Forgot," offered Charlie, shortly. "Bought it on the way out and forgot."

"Even though it's wrapped in underwear you packed last night?" accused the official. He made them unpack all their luggage, searching it slowly, so their departure would be delayed. If his dinner was going to be ruined, so would their homecoming.

"It'll cost you £4 in duty," he said, finally, surveying their wrecked suitcases.

It was another hour before they reached the M3 on the way to London.

"Sometimes," said Edith, breaking the silence, "I really don't understand you, Charlie."

"Bullshit," he said.

6

Cuthbertson had telephoned ahead, so Snare and Harrison were already waiting in the office when the Director and Wilberforce flurried in from their meeting with the Cabinet. It was the first occasion it had happened and he'd impressed them. Cuthbertson knew. There'd be other meetings at Downing Street, after today.

Cuthbertson was purple-faced with excitement, smiling for no reason, moving round the room without direction, nerves too tight to permit him to sit down.

"Everyone agrees," he announced, generally. He giggled, stupidly. The other three men pretended not to notice.

Since the disaster of the Berenkov debriefing, Cuthbertson had always waited for an independent judgment. With Kalenin, he had insisted on two assessments and then met with the Foreign Secretary before bringing it before the full cabinet. The Prime Minister had been incredibly flattering, remembered Cuthbertson. He felt warm and knew his blood pressure would be dangerously high.

"This is going to be the sensation of the year . . . any year," insisted Cuthbertson, as if challenging a denial. He looked at the others in the office. Wilberforce probed his pipe. Snare and Harrison nodded agreement.

"Kalenin didn't actually say anything about defection, did he?" queried Snare, selecting a bad moment.

Cuthbertson stared at the man as if he had emitted an offensive smell.

"Good Lord, man, of course not. But you've read the Moscow reports from Colonel Wilcox. He used to be in my regiment . . . know the man's integrity as well as I know my own. There can be only one possible interpretation."

"So what happens now?" asked Harrison, pleased at the rebuff to Snare.

"He's given us our lead. Now we've got to follow it."

"How?" said Snare, anxious to recover.

"The Queen's Birthday," declared Cuthbertson, quickly, leaning back in his chair and smiling up at the ceiling.

Christ, it was better than soldiering, he thought.

"There's going to be a party at the Moscow embassy to celebrate it. And there's the Leipzig Fair."

Snare frowned, but stayed silent. He could easily understand how the General annoyed Charles Muffin, he thought.

"If Kalenin turns up at either, we'll get our proof."

"I don't quite see . . ." Wilberforce stumbled.

"Because we'll be at both places, to speak to him," enlarged the Director.

"Are you sure he'll go to Leipzig? It'll be unusual attending a trade affair, surely?" questioned Harrison.

Irritably, Cuthbertson rummaged in the file, extracting the report from the trade counsellor at the Moscow embassy that had accompanied that of the military attaché.

". . . 'Trade is important between our two countries,' " quoted the Director. ". . . 'I personally hope to see it first hand at this year's convention . . . Through trade, there will be peace, not war . . .' "

He looked up, fixing Harrison, who shifted uncomfortably.

". . . Where's the Easter trade delegation?" he demanded, needlessly. "Leipzig, of course."

"Will we be able to get visas in time?" smirked Snare.

"There's a vacancy on the embassy establishment in

Moscow," said Cuthbertson, airily. "It'll be easy to get you accredited."

Colour began to suffuse Snare's face.

"So I'm going to Moscow?" he clarified.

"Of course," said Cuthbertson. "And Harrison to East Germany."

He gazed at Snare. "Wilcox is a good man . . . he'll cooperate fully," predicted the Director.

Neither operative looked enthusiastic.

"This is going to stamp our control indelibly upon the service," continued Cuthbertson. "We'll be the envy of every country in the West . . . they'll come to us cap in hand for any crumbs we can spare . . ."

"It won't be easy," said Harrison. It would be disastrous if he made a mistake, he thought. Fleetingly the vision of the burning Volkswagen and the body he had thought to be that of Charles Muffin flickered into his mind.

"Of course it won't be easy. The Russians will do anything to prevent Kalenin from leaving . . ." agreed Cuthbertson. He paused, looking carefully from one to the other. ". . . You'll have to be bloody careful. Let Kalenin make the moves all the time."

"And if he doesn't?"

The hope in Snare's voice was evident to everyone in the room.

"Then you'll stay in Moscow for a few months until we can withdraw you without it being too obvious. And Harrison can come out when the Fair is over."

"If nothing happens," enthused Harrison, later, as the two operatives sat in the office formerly occupied by Charlie Muffin, "think of all the wonderful ballet you'll be able to see. I hear the Bolshoi are marvellous."

Snare stayed gazing out of the window into Whitehall. At least those killed in the war had a public monument, he thought, looking at the Cenotaph.

"I don't like ballet," he said bitterly.

Back in Cuthbertson's office, Janet carried in the carefully brewed Earl Grey tea, placing the transparent bone china cups gently alongside the Director and Wilberforce, then returned within minutes with two plates, each containing four chocolate digestive biscuits.

She stood, waiting.

"What is it?" demanded Cuthbertson, impatiently.

"I thought you might have forgotten," offered Janet. "Mr. Muffin returned this morning. He's been in the office, all day."

"Oh Christ!" said Cuthbertson. He stared at Wilberforce, deciding to delegate. Muffin wasn't important any more.

"You see him," he ordered the second man.

"What shall I tell him to do?"

Cuthbertson shrugged, dismissively, taking care to break his biscuits so that no crumbs fell away from the plate.

"Oh, I don't know," he said, consumed by the Kalenin development. "Let him see Berenkov again."

"So Muffin isn't to be demoted?" probed Wilberforce, anxious to avoid being blamed for another mistake.

The Director paused, tea-cup to his lips.

"Of course he is," he snapped, definitely. Even though the man had been right, showing them the way to uncover three other members of Berenkov's system, Cuthbertson didn't intend admitting the error.

"But for God's sake, man, consider the priority," he insisted. "The last thing that matters is somebody as unimportant as Muffin. Kalenin is the only consideration now."

Charlie lay exhausted in the darkness, feeling the sweat dry coldly upon him. He hooked his feet under the slippery sheet, trying to drag it over him, finally unclasping his hands from behind his head to complete the task. He didn't like silk bed-linen, he decided.

"So he won't even see me?" he said.

"He's very busy," defended Janet, loyally, intrigued by the self-pity in Charlie's voice. She hoped he wasn't going to become a bore: she'd almost decided to take him to a party the coming Saturday, to show him to her friends.

"What's happening?" asked Charlie turning to her. In the darkness, she wouldn't detect his attention.

"There's a hell of a flap," reported the girl. "We're trying to get Snare a visa for Moscow. And Harrison into East Germany under Department of Trade cover for the Leipzig Fair."

"Why?"

"Cuthbertson thinks some General or Colonel or something wants to defect from Russia."

"Who?"

"He won't identify him. Even the memorandum to the Prime Minister refers to the man by code."

Charlie smiled in the darkness. The bloody fools.

"You'll be annoyed tomorrow, Charlie," predicted the girl, suddenly.

He waited.

"Remember the last time you saw Berenkov . . . the day your shoes leaked . . . ?"

"Yes."

"Cuthbertson has cut the taxi fare off your expenses. He dictated a memo today, saying you'd obviously walked."

The girl went silent, expecting an angry reaction. Instead she detected him laughing and smiled, too. Charlie was such an unpredictable man, she thought, fondly. She *would* take him to Jennifer's 21st.

"I *did* miss you, Charlie."

"Yes," he said, distantly, his mind on other things.

"Charlie."

"What?"

"Make love to me again . . . the way I like it . . ."

The trouble with her preference, thought Charlie, pushing the sheet away, was that he always got cramp in his legs.

He sighed. And it was going to be a cold walk home, he thought. He'd been relying on those expenses: now he couldn't afford a taxi.

7

Hesitant and uncomfortable, like a couple selected by a computer dating service, the two Directors finally met at Cuthbertson's club in St. James's Street, agreeing on its security. Each had had detailed biographies prepared by their services on the other, and had memorised them. Purposely, phrases were introduced into the small talk, showing the preparation, each wanting the other to know that he was aware it wasn't really a social occasion.

He'd been right, decided Ruttgers, smiling across the lunch table at the man. Sir Henry Cuthbertson was lost outside the barrack square and the benefit of Queen's Regulations.

The Kalenin approach had been made at an American embassy function, recalled Cuthbertson, answering the smile. Their awareness and the consequent approach was hardly surprising. That the Director had come from Washington was unexpected, though. He'd impress Ruttgers, like he'd impressed the Prime Minister, three weeks earlier, determined the Briton.

"These Arbroath smokies are very good," complimented the American, boning the smoked fish. "It's something we don't have in America."

"I'm very fond of your cherry-stone clams," countered Cuthbertson. Advantage Cuthbertson, he decided.

"I was very glad when the Secretary of State suggested I come to make your acquaintance."

The American lifted the Chablis at the end of the sentence.

"Cheers."

"Cheers," accepted Cuthbertson. "Yes, liaison is very important."

"Vitally important," said Ruttgers.

Deuce, decided Cuthbertson, irritably.

The waiter came to clear the plates, saving him.

"In every field," he generalised.

"But I'm interested in one particular aspect," pressed Ruttgers. "The immediate future plans of a certain General."

Cuthbertson stared around him, alarmed. He was going to lose the encounter, he thought, worriedly.

The artificial reaction amused the American, who waited until the other man had come back to him. This was going to be comparatively easy, thought Ruttgers.

"We know all about it," exaggerated the C.I.A. chief. "We know you're expecting further contact within a week or two."

It had been easy in the closed environment of Moscow to discover the impending arrival of the man named Snare. Already, the operative who had been Braley's deputy in the Soviet capital had been ordered to keep the Briton under permanent observation once he arrived. They'd know immediately if there was a move, Ruttgers hoped.

"I find it difficult to understand what you're talking about," said Cuthbertson, stiffly. This wasn't going at all like the Downing Street meeting. No one had pushed him then, just listened in polite attention.

"Come now, Sir Henry," protested Ruttgers, lightly, carefully lifting the mollusc from the top of his steak and kidney pudding and frowning at it.

"It's an oyster," said the Briton helpfully. "You're supposed to eat it with the pudding."

Ruttgers pushed it to the side of his plate.

"There is no other man in the world to whom I would dream of talking as directly as this," continued Ruttgers, flatteringly, holding Cuthbertson's eyes in a gaze of honesty. "We don't have to be coy with each other, surely?"

Cuthbertson speared several marinated kidneys, filling his mouth so he could avoid an immediate reaction. The other man's directness flustered him, as it was intended to do.

"There *is* a development in the East which is quite interesting," conceded the Briton, at last. He sipped his Château Latour reflectively. "And I'm sure you won't be offended," he hurried on, disclosing his apprehension, "when I say I don't see that at the moment it affects you in the slightest . . ."

He paused, growing bolder.

". . . There is an excellent liaison between us, as we have agreed. If anything transpires, you'll hear about it through the normal channels."

Damned prig, thought Ruttgers, smiling broadly in open friendship. He hadn't believed people talked of "normal channels" any more.

"Sir Henry," he placated, "let's not misunderstand each other."

"I don't think there's any misunderstanding," insisted Cuthbertson. The game was swinging back his way, he decided.

Ruttgers spread his hands, recognising the dead end.

"The Kalenin affair is spectacular," he announced, selecting a different path and trying to shock the man into concessions.

Cuthbertson curbed any concern this time.

"It really is too much for one service," said the American.

"I can recommend the Stilton," said Cuthbertson, twisting away. "With a glass of Taylors, perhaps?"

Ruttgers nodded his acceptance, feeling the anger surface. Arrogant, stupid old bastard. How, he wondered, desperately, would the professional soldier react to the suggestion of higher authority?

"I have it on the direct instructions of the President himself," disclosed Ruttgers, grandly, "that I can offer the full and complete services of the C.I.A. on this operation."

"That's very nice," replied Cuthbertson.

The American was unsure whether he was referring to the offer or the cheese.

"It would be an absolute disaster for the West if anything went wrong," bullied Ruttgers.

"I'm quite confident nothing will," said Cuthbertson, dabbing his lips with the linen napkin. The two men sat looking at each other.

"I shall be staying in London for some time," said Ruttgers, maintaining the smile. "Now that we've opened up this personal contact between our two services, I think it should continue."

"Oh," prompted Cuthbertson, uncertainly.

"By regular meetings," expanded Ruttgers.

"Of course," agreed the British Director, surprised that the other man had capitulated so easily. "I'd like that."

And he would, decided Cuthbertson, leaving the club for his waiting car. People appeared remarkably easy to handle: this job wasn't going to be as difficult as he had feared, after all.

He smiled, settling back against the leather upholstery. It had been game, set and match, he decided.

The greetings weren't the same any more, recognised Charlie, as Berenkov entered the interview room. The Russian's exuberance was strained, as if he were constantly having to force his attitude and recall the exaggerated gestures. His skin had that grey, shining look of a man deprived of fresh air for a long period, and the familiar mane of hair was flecked with grey, too. The prison denims were freshly laundered and pressed, but the hands that lay flaccid on the table between them were rough, the once immaculate nails chipped and rimmed with dirt.

"It's good of you to come so often, Charlie," thanked Berenkov.

Since his return from holiday, Charlie had visited the spy every week: the decline in that time could be almost measured on a graph, thought the Briton.

"How is it?" Charlie asked, concerned.

Berenkov shrugged. He sat hunched over the table, as if he were guarding something between his fingers. Charlie saw the palm of his right hand was nicotine-stained where he smoked in the prison fashion, cigarette cupped inwards against detection. A year ago, thought Charlie, Berenkov had had a gold holder for the Havana Havanas. The Russian appeared to notice the dirtiness of his nails for the first time and began trying to pick away the dirt.

"It's not easy to adjust to a place like this, Charlie."

"You'll get used to it," said Charlie, immediately offended by his own platitude.

Berenkov looked directly at him for the first time, a sad expression.

"I'm sorry," apologised Charlie. He should be careful to avoid banal remarks, he decided.

"What's happening outside?" asked Berenkov.

"It's a rotten spring," replied Charlie. "More like winter—bloody cold and wet."

"I used to like the English winters," said Berenkov, nostalgically. "Some Sundays I used to go to Bournemouth and walk along the seafront, watching the sand driven over the promenade by the sea."

Bournemouth, noted Charlie. Too far for a casual afternoon stroll. So Berenkov had had a source at the Navy's Underwater Weapons Establishment at Portland. He'd have to submit a report to Cuthbertson: they thought they had plugged the leak by the arrest of Houghton and Gee after the detection of Lonsdale, back in the 1960s.

"You've been taken off the active rota," challenged Berenkov, unexpectedly.

Charlie smiled. The Russian wasn't completely numbed by his imprisonment, he thought. But it was a fairly obvious deduction from the frequency of the visits.

"I suppose so," admitted Charlie.

"What happened?"

"Face didn't fit," reported the Briton. "There was a new regime: I upset them."

The Russian carefully examined the man sitting before him, easily able to understand how he could have offended the British caste system.

Charlie Muffin was the sort of man whose shirt tail always escaped from his trousers, like a rude tongue.

Apart from the flat-vowelled accent, Charlie wore his fair hair too long and without any style, flopped back from his forehead. He perspired easily and thus rarely looked washed and the fading collars of his shirts sat uncomfortably over a haphazardly knotted tie, so it was possible to see that the top button was missing. It was a department store suit, bagged and shapeless from daily wearing, the pockets bulging like a schoolboy's with unseen things stored in readiness for a use that never arose.

Yet about this man, decided the Russian, there was the indefinable ambience of ruthless toughness he had detected among the long-term prisoners with whom he was having daily contact. In Charlie it was cloaked by an over-all impression of down-at-the-heels shabbiness. But it was definitely there.

It was almost impossible to believe the man possessed such an incredible mind, thought Berenkov.

"Is it a change for the good?" asked the Russian.

The recorders were probably still operating, thought Charlie, despite the lack of interest now in Berenkov.

"They've a different approach," sidestepped Charlie. "Very regimental."

"Soldiers can't run spy systems," declared Berenkov, positively, picking up the clue that Charlie had offered.

"You're a General," said Charlie. "And so is Kalenin."

"Honorary titles, really," said the Russian, easily. He seemed to brighten. "More for the salary scale and emoluments than for anything else."

"Just like the capitalist societies," picked up Charlie, noting the change of attitude. "Every job has got its perks."

The Russian became serious again.

"You haven't forgotten what I said, Charlie," he

urged, reaching across the table and seizing the other man's wrist. "Be careful . . . even though they've pushed you aside, be careful."

Charlie freed his wrist, embarrassed.

"I'll be all right," he said. He sounded like a child protesting his bravery in the dark, he thought.

The Russian stared around the interview room.

"Don't ever let yourself get put in jail," he said, very seriously.

"I won't," agreed Charlie, too easily.

"I mean it," insisted Berenkov. "If you get jailed, Charlie, your lot wouldn't bother to get you out. Kill yourself rather than get caught."

Charlie frowned at the statement. He would have thought Berenkov could have withstood the loss of freedom better than this. He felt suddenly frightened and wanted to leave the prison.

"Come again?" pleaded Berenkov.

"If I can," said Charlie, as he always did. At the door he turned, on impulse. Berenkov was standing in the middle of the room, shoulders bowed, gazing after him. There was a look of enormous sadness on his face.

"Charlie," he told himself, waiting in du Cane Road for the bus. "You're getting too arrogant. And arrogance breeds carelessness."

A woman in the line looked at him curiously. She'd seen his lips move, Charlie realised.

"So it didn't work?" queried Braley, perched on the windowsill of the room that had been made available to them in the American embassy in Grosvenor Square.

"No," snapped Ruttgers. His face burned with anger. "Pompous s.o.b. spent most of the time trying to teach me how to eat oysters."

Braley frowned, trying to understand, but said nothing.

"We can't do anything unless they let us in," said the Moscow Resident.

"I know," agreed Ruttgers, slowly.

"So what now?" asked Braley.

Ruttgers smiled, an expression entirely devoid of humour.

"Lean on them," said the Director. "In every way."

Braley waited, expectantly.

"And if something started happening to their operatives," continued Ruttgers, "then they'd need assistance, wouldn't they?"

"Yes," agreed Braley. "They would."

Ruttgers, he thought, looking at the mild little man, was a rare sort of bastard. It was right to be frightened of him.

8

General Valery Kalenin entered the Leipzig Convention Hall at precisely 11:15 A.M. on March 11. Harrison noted the exact time, determined to prepare an impeccable report to Cuthbertson on his first absolutely solo operation. A bubble of excitement formed in his stomach and he bunched his hands in his pockets, trying to curtail the shaking.

The Russian was in plain clothes, a neat, fussy little figure who appeared to listen constantly, but say hardly anything. The deference towards him was very obvious, Harrison saw.

The General moved in the middle of a body of men, three of whom Harrison had seen during the previous two days at the Fair. The recognition annoyed him: he hadn't isolated them as secret policemen. One had got quite drunk at the opening ceremony and Harrison had marked the three as relaxing communist businessmen. The episode would have been a ploy, he realised now, a clever attempt to tempt people into unconsidered words or action. The mistake worried him. Charles Muffin would have probably recognised them.

Kalenin appeared in no hurry, hesitating at exhibition stands and closely examining products. Any questions, Harrison noted, were usually addressed through one of the other people in the party, so avoiding direct contact.

Harrison's entry documents described him as an export specialist in the Department of Trade and Industry, enabling him free movement to any British exhibition. Impatiently, he shifted between the stalls and platforms, accepting the nods and smiles of recognition; with the obedience instilled by his army training, he had dutifully followed instructions and befriended those businessmen providing his cover.

"Let Kalenin take the lead"—He recalled Cuthbertson's orders, watching the agonisingly slow progress of the Russian party, but holding back from direct approach. It would have been impossible to achieve anyway, he thought: there needed to be an excuse for the meeting to prevent surprise in the rest of the party.

At noon, by Harrison's close time-keeping, Kalenin was only two stalls away, lingering with the Australian exhibitors. The Briton imagined he detected growing attention from the diminutive, squat man at the approach to the British section. Harrison positioned himself away from the first display, an office equipment stand, remaining near an exhibit of farm machinery. It comprised tractors and harvesters, among which it was possible for a man to remain inconspicuous, Harrison reasoned.

At the office equipment stall, Kalenin abandoned for the first time the practice of talking through the men with him, instead posing direct questions to the stallholders.

"Wants to show off his English," commented the salesman by Harrison's side. The operative turned sideways, smiling. The man's name was Dalton or Walton, he thought. Prided himself as a wit and had spent the previous evening telling blue jokes at the convention hotel.

"Any idea who he is?" floated Harrison.

"Looks important from the entourage," guessed the salesman.

Harrison went back to the Russian party, detecting movement, but the farm machinery salesman was ahead of him, beaming.

"Reminds me of a T-54," Kalenin said hopefully, pointing to a combine harvester and looking to his companions in anticipation. There was a scattering of smiles and Kalenin appeared disappointed at the response.

"But more useful than a tank, surely, sir," intruded Harrison, seeing the blank look on the stallholder's face.

Kalenin stared directly at him, gratefully.

"Do you know tanks?" asked the General. "They're a hobby of mine."

"Only of them," said Harrison.

"A man of peace, not war," judged the Russian, smiling.

"A man whom my country much admires, once remarked that through trade there will be peace, not war . . ." tried Harrison, quickly, wondering if the man would remember quoted verbatim what he had said at the American embassy reception. If Kalenin missed the significance, he would have to be more direct and that would be dangerous in such an open situation.

Harrison was conscious of a very intense examination. Please God, don't let him misconstrue it, thought the Englishman.

"A wise comment," accepted Kalenin.

He *had* remembered, decided Harrison. He felt very nervous, aware that the attention of the entire party was upon them and that the tractor salesman was desperately attempting to edge back into the conversation, believing Kalenin to be a trade official. The man thrust forward a square of pasteboard eagerly.

"Bolton, sir," he introduced. "Joseph Bolton."

"And a remark my country remembered," over-rode Harrison, desperate not to lose the opportunity. He was attempting to reduce the sound of his voice, so it would not be heard by the others.

"Perhaps there should be a wider exchange of views between the two?" suggested Kalenin.

"They're looking forward very eagerly to such a possibility," responded Harrison. Elation swept through him. The last time he had experienced such a sensation, he remembered, was when he had collected his Double First at university and seen his parents, who had been separated for ten years, holding hands and crying.

He'd done it, he knew. In four minutes of apparently innocuous banter, he had brilliantly achieved what he had been sent to do.

Kalenin turned to the salesman, accepting the card at last. None of the others would have suspected anything, decided Harrison. It was perfect.

"Show me the engine," said Kalenin, then immediately proceeded to ask three technical questions showing his knowledge of machinery. The visit was consummately timed, assessed Harrison, admiringly. The Russian allowed exactly the proper amount of attention before disengaging himself to move back into the group.

"It was a pleasant meeting, sir," said Harrison, walking with him towards the edge of the stand. "Perhaps on another occasion?"

"I don't know," countered Kalenin. "I'm leaving Leipzig tonight."

The Russian spoke in the short, precise sentences of a dedicated man who had learned English in a language laboratory.

"It would be nice, possibly, to extend the conversation," said Harrison, dangerously.

"Yes. I'd like that," replied Kalenin, already moving on.

Harrison stood, savouring the knowledge of success, watching the party involve themselves in other displays. From no one came a backward glance that would have hinted suspicion.

"If you'd spend less time getting in the bloody way, I might have made some progress there."

Harrison turned to the annoyed salesman: Bolton, he remembered.

"He took your card, Mr. Bolton," pointed out Harrison.

"You damned D.T.I. men are all the same," went on Bolton, unmollified. "Out for a bloody social occasion.

Some of us live by selling, not as parasites off the tax-payer."

Harrison was conscious of the amused attention of the adjacent stalls and smiled. Nothing could upset him after the preceding fifteen minutes.

"He devoted more time to you than any other English exhibit," offered Harrison, moving away.

"For bloody nothing," echoed behind him.

Harrison spent the afternoon preparing a verbatim transcript of the encounter, sipping frequently from the duty-free whisky he'd bought on the outward journey and which he felt he deserved, in celebration. Charlie Muffin, whom everybody had considered so damned good, couldn't have done as well, he convinced himself, belching and grimacing at the fumes that rose in his throat. The whole meeting had been magnificent; it didn't matter if the others with Kalenin had heard every word. To anyone but the two of them, it was just a meaningless exchange of pleasantries.

He felt quite light-headed when he located the rest of the government party and entrusted the security-sealed envelope to the courier for transmission to the East Berlin embassy and then the diplomatic bag to London next day.

He had a five-day holiday, he realised, suddenly, sitting in the hotel bar that evening. He looked around the drab room. Hardly the place he would have chosen to spend it.

In the far corner, Bolton was in his accustomed role, the centre of a raucous group and involved in a story which needed much hand-waving.

Harrison smiled and nodded, but the tractor-salesman pointedly ignored him.

The C.I.A. cover for the Fair was through a legitimate firm of timber exporters based in Vancouver, British Columbia. From their observer, five stools further down the bar, had already gone the report of the unexpected presence that day of General Kalenin, following Ruttgers's alert to all Warsaw Pact stations to react immediately to the appearance of the man whose face they knew after twenty-five years' anonymity.

"Bolton's bloody angry," reported the Australian with the stall adjoining the British office equipment exhibit, nodding along the bar.

"Why?" asked the C.I.A. man, politely. The Australian's tendency to drink beer until he was sick offended the American.

"Reckons the bloody man screwed up an order from that important-looking Russian delegation that came through this morning?"

The C.I.A. man looked towards Harrison with growing interest.

"Who is he?" asked the American.

The Australian, who had served in Vietnam and retained the vernacular like a medal, wanting people to recognise it, moved closer and affirmed, "I reckon a spook . . . a bleedin' spook. From the questions he's been asking the exhibitors, he knows fuck all about trade."

"Excuse me," said the C.I.A. man. "Reports to write for head office."

Four days later, Harrison set off alone in a hired Skoda, driving slowly, unsure of the way, wishing within an hour of departure he had curbed his boredom and returned in convoy with the main British contingent.

He was moving along the wide, tree-lined highway about twenty miles outside of East Berlin when he first became conscious of the following car in his rear-view mirror. It was too far away to determine the number of occupants and Harrison kept glancing at the reflection, expecting it to overtake. It appeared to be keeping a regular distance and Harrison experienced the first jerk of fear. Immediately he subdued it; his trade cover was perfect and he carried no incriminating material whatsoever. There couldn't be the slightest danger.

So occupied was he with what was following that for those first few seconds Harrison thought the traffic ahead had slowed because of an accident. Then he realised it was a road block. He recognised soldiers as

well as People's Police and saw that in addition to the
vans that completely closed the highway, strips of
spiked metal had been laid zigzag in front of them, to
rip out the tyres of any vehicle that didn't slow to less
than walking pace to negotiate the barrier.

Then he realised the following car had closed behind
him. There were only five yards between them now and
he could see five men jammed uncomfortably in the
other vehicle.

"Oh, my God," said Harrison aloud.

In the first few seconds of unthinking confusion, he
braked, accelerated, then braked again, so that the car
leapfrogged towards the obstruction. Two soldiers in
front of the spikes motioned him to stop and men began fanning out along either side of the road. The
recollection of the burning Volkswagen and the dull,
thudding sound that the bullets had made, hitting the
body, forced itself into his mind and again he braked,
sharply and with design this time, trying to spin the car
in its own length so that he could be facing back up
the road. The vehicle stuck, halfway around, pointing
uselessly towards the bordering field. To his right, Harrison saw the following car had anticipated the manœuvre and turned across the road, blocking any retreat.

Harrison was sobbing now, the breath shuddering
from him. There was no reason why he should be de-
tained, he assured himself, his lips moving. No reason.
Or excuse. Don't panic. Act in the outraged manner of
any important government official irritated by being
stopped. The car episode was easily explained; just dis-
miss it as lack of control in an emergency situation in a
rented car.

He thrust out of the vehicle and began walking pur-
posefully towards the road block, protest disordered in
his mind. But then he saw the uniforms and fear got
control of him and he stopped. His mouth opened, but
no sound emerged. And then he ran, stupidly, first
towards the waiting soldiers, then sideways, trying to
leap the ditch.

There was no sound of warning before the firing, which came almost casually from a machine gun mounted on a pivot near the driving position of the leading armoured car. Harrison was hit in mid-air and dropped, quite silently, into the ditch he was trying to leap.

The driver and one of the men from the following car walked slowly up the road, hands buried into the pockets of their leather topcoats, breath forming tiny clouds in front of them as they walked. For several minutes they stood staring down into the ditch, alert for any movement that would indicate he was still alive. Only Harrison's legs were visible, the rest of him submerged in the black, leaf-covered water. His foot jerked spasmodically, furrowing a tiny groove in the opposite bank. It only lasted a few seconds and then it was quite still.

"It's not possible to spin a Skoda like that," said the driver, as they turned to go back to their own vehicle.

"No?"

"No. Something to do with the suspension and the angle that the wheels are splayed."

"Must be safe on ice, then?"

"I suppose so."

"We won't tell Snare," decreed Cuthbertson. He stood at the window, watching a snake of tourists slowly enter the Houses of Parliament. They were Japanese, he saw, armoured in camera equipment and wearing coloured lapel pins identifying them with their guides, who carried corresponding standards in greens and reds and yellows.

"All right," agreed Wilberforce.

"It would be quite wrong," justified Cuthbertson, turning back into the room. "He'd go to Moscow frightened. A frightened man can't be expected to operate properly. It's basic training."

"Need he go at all?" asked Wilberforce. "Surely Harrison's report is pretty conclusive."

"Oh yes," insisted Cuthbertson. "He's got to go. I'm

convinced now, but we need to know the conditions that Kalenin will impose. And if he's made his own escape plans. A man like Kalenin won't just walk into an embassy and give himself up."

"Yes," concurred Wilberforce. "I suppose you're right."

They remained silent while Janet served the tea. It was several minutes after she had left the office before the conversation resumed.

"Was it a surprise?" asked Wilberforce, nodding to the door through which the girl had left the room.

"What?" demanded Cuthbertson, pretending not to know what the other man was talking about.

"To discover from the security reports that Janet was having an affair with that man Muffin."

"Not really," lied the Director. "I gather he has a reputation for that sort of thing. Rutting always has been the pastime of the working class."

He shook his head, like a man confused with a distasteful sight.

"Imagine!" he invited. "With someone like that!"

"What are you going to do?" asked the second-in-command. "He's married and she's the daughter of a fellow officer, for God's sake."

Cuthbertson opened the other file on his desk, containing the report of Harrison's death.

"Let's see how Snare gets on," he said guardedly.

"Over six months have passed since Comrade General Berenkov was sentenced," recorded Kastanazy, gazing over his desk at Kalenin.

"Yes," said the K.G.B. officer.

"Most of yesterday's Praesidium meeting was devoted to discussing the affair."

"Yes," said the General.

"Please understand, Comrade Kalenin, that the patience of everyone is growing increasingly shorter."

"Yes," agreed the General.

Had Kastanazy purposely dropped his rank? he wondered.

9

Snare hated Moscow, he decided. It was claustro-
phobic and petty-minded and inefficient and irritating.
He had attended the Bolshoi and been unmoved, the
State Circus and been bored and the Armoury and
been unimpressed with the Romanov jewellery, even
the Fabergé clocks. The body of Lenin, enclosed behind glass in that mausoleum, was not, he had concluded, the embalmed body at all, but a wax-work.
And a bad wax-work at that. He'd seen better at
Madame Tussaud's, when he'd taken his young nephew
for an Easter outing. The child had wet himself, he
remembered, distastefully, and made the car smell.

The flattery of being lionised as a new face in an
embassy starved of outside contact had worn off now
and he pitied the diplomats and secretaries whose constant opening gambit was to refer to his thoughtfulness
in bringing as gifts from London, Heinz baked beans,
Walls pork sausages and Fortnum & Mason Guinness
cake. It had been Muffin's advice, recalled Snare. Just
the sort of sycophantic rubbish in which the man
would have indulged, a gesture to make people like
him.

He'd spent several evenings with the Director's
friend, Colonel Wilcox, and rehearsed their approach if
Kalenin attended the official function. But even Wilcox
had erected a barrier, afraid any mistake could create
an embarrassing diplomatic incident. So no one liked
him, decided Snare. He didn't give a damn. Thank
Christ, he thought, gazing out of the embassy window,
that the stupid party was tonight and he could start

thinking of his return to London. It was raining heavily, smearing the houses and roads with a dull, grey colour. It was hardly surprising, he thought, that the Russians seemed so miserable.

The interest of the Americans slightly worried him. They knew who he was, he accepted. That absurdly tall man who kept talking about basket-ball, moving his hands in a flopping motion as if he were bouncing a ball against the ground, was definitely an Agency man. Snare groped for the man's name, but had forgotten it. Odd how sportsmen liked to boast their chosen recreation, he considered. Harrison was always driving imaginary golf balls with his reversed umbrella.

Someone in the British embassy must have disclosed his identity, he thought. When he got back to London, he'd complain to Sir Henry Cuthbertson and get an investigation ordered. Bloody diplomats were all the same: trying to show off their knowledge, gossiping their secrets.

The fact that he was known to be an operative didn't matter, he rationalised. They'd be expecting him to do something befitting his role and all he had to do was attend an embassy party and, if Kalenin were there, carry on where Harrison had left the conversation in East Germany.

And because no one, apart from the British, knew what that conversation was, then all he would appear to be doing was behaving in a normal, social manner.

The thought of achieving his mission while they all watched, unaware of what was happening, amused him. It would have been pleasant, letting them know, afterwards how stupid they had been. But probably dangerous. He sighed, abandoning the idea.

Snare turned away from the window, taking from the desk immediately behind it the coded report that had come from Whitehall three weeks earlier giving a complete account of Harrison's meeting with the General.

Harrison had done bloody well, congratulated Snare. When he got back to London, he'd take the man out for a celebration meal, to l'Étoile or l'Épicure. Some decent food would be welcome after what he had endured for the past month, when he'd been lucky enough to get any service at all in a hotel or restaurant.

Carefully, he traced the responses that Kalenin had given in Leipzig. There could be no doubt, he agreed, turning to Cuthbertson's assessment, that the General was a potential defector. The East German encounter had shown him the pathway, thought Snare. But it was still going to be difficult if Kalenin turned up, discovering the undoubted conditions that the man would impose. Secretly he hoped Kalénin wouldn't appear: then he could just go home. Yes, he thought, it would be better if Kalenin didn't attend. Because whatever he achieved tonight, if anything at all, would be secondary to Harrison's initial success. It was bloody unfair, thought Snare, irritably, that the other man had just got six days in East Germany and all the glory and he'd been stuck in Moscow for four weeks and had to perform the most difficult part of the whole operation.

He descended early to the ballroom, arriving with the first of the British party. He spoke briefly to the ambassador and Colonel Wilcox, discussed the quality of the Cambridge eight with the cultural attaché who had been his senior at King's and had got a rowing blue, and then edged away, to be alone. Being disliked had its advantages, he thought: no one bothered to follow.

The American contingent arrived early and there were more of them than Snare had expected. What an appalling life, sympathised Snare, playing follow-my-leader from one embassy gathering to another, repeating the same conversations like a litany and attempting to keep sane. Almost immediately behind the Americans, the rest of the diplomatic corps arrived, crushing into the entrance and slowly funnelling past the hosts towards the drinks tray and tables of canapés. Whatever did these people, all of whom had seen each other in the last week and to which absolutely nothing had happened in the interim, find to talk about? wondered the Briton.

At the far end of the chandeliered room, an orchestra was attempting Gilbert and Sullivan and Snare was reminded of the amateur musical society at his prep school.

"Hi."

Snare turned to the fat man who had appeared at his elbow. He seemed to be experiencing some difficulty in his breathing.

"Braley," the man introduced. "American embassy."

Another C.I.A. man? wondered the Briton.

"Hello," he returned, minimally.

"Could be a good party."

Snare looked at him, but didn't bother to reply.

"Not seen you before. Been in Washington on leave, myself."

"I envy you," said Snare, with feeling.

"Don't you like Moscow?"

"No."

"How long will you be stationed here?"

"As briefly as possible," said Snare.

Christ, thought Braley. And the man was supposed to have diplomatic cover: hadn't anyone briefed him?

"Believe you've met my colleague, Jim Cox?" said Braley, brightly.

Snare looked at the second American and nodded. He wasn't practising his basket approach tonight, Snare saw. What had really offended him about Cox, a thin-faced, urgent-demeanoured man who did callisthenics every morning and jogged, according to his own confession, for an hour in the U.S. embassy compound in the afternoon, was the discovery that the price he was offering Snare for the duty-free, embassy-issued Scotch would have only allowed a profit of twenty pence a bottle. The offence was not monetary, but the knowledge that others in the embassy would have learned about it and laughed at him for being gullible, particularly after the apparent well-travelled act of bringing in the beans and sausages. Everyone would know now that it wasn't his idea, but somebody else's. They'd probably guess Charlie Muffin, he thought; in his first few days in the Soviet capital, there had been several friendly enquiries about the bloody man.

Snare looked back to Braley. So he was an Agency man too. Best not to encourage them.

"Excuse me," said Snare, edging away. "I've just seen somebody I must talk to."

"An idiot," judged Braley, watching the Englishman disappear through the crowd.

"I told you he wasn't liked," reminded Cox. Apart from the invisible basket-ball practice, Cox had the habit of rising and falling on the balls of his feet, to strengthen his calf muscles. He did it now and Braley frowned with annoyance. Cox would probably die of a heart attack when he was forty.

"I thought you were exaggerating," confessed Braley. "He's unbelievable."

"It's been like this all the time."

"The Director said there had been changes. I wasn't aware how bad their service had got. They certainly need our involvement."

Cox dropped an imagined ball perfectly through the shade of a wall light, nodding seriously to his superior.

"The Russians *must* have spotted him," he predicted.

Braley looked at him, sadly.

"They know us *all*," he cautioned. "Don't . . ."

"Here he is," broke off Cox, urgently.

Braley stopped talking, looking towards the entrance. There were ten in the Russian party. Kalenin was the last to come through the door, separated from the others by a gap of about five yards. He wore a uniform, which seemed to engulf him, and moved awkwardly, as if uncomfortable among so many people.

Politely he stood last in line as his colleagues eased forward, greeting the ambassador and the assembled diplomatic corps.

"And there goes Snare," completed Cox, needlessly. The Englishman had positioned himself near the side table laid out with cocktail snacks. He moved away as the Russians entered, remaining halfway between it and the greeting officials, permitting him a second chance of an encounter, as they came to eat, if Colonel Wilcox failed to hold Kalenin sufficiently for the rehearsed meeting.

But Wilcox didn't fail. Soldierly obedient to his instructions, the distinguished, moustached officer immediately moved to engage Kalenin, and Snare continued forward. He estimated he had ten minutes in which to confirm absolutely the conviction about the Russian General by discovering the conditions.

Wilcox saw his expected approach and smiled, half turning in feigned invitation. It was going almost too well, thought Snare, apprehensively, entering the group.

"General, I don't believe you've met the newest recruit to our embassy, Brian Snare."

The Englishman waited, uncertain whether to extend his hand. Kalenin gave a stiff little bow, nodding his head.

Befitting the Gilbert and Sullivan string ensemble, decided Snare, answering the bow.

"A pleasure, General," he began. It would, he guessed, be another fencing session, like that which Harrison had recorded so well from East Germany.

"And mine," responded the Russian.

"Your command of English is remarkably good," praised Snare, seeking an opening. He glanced almost imperceptibly at Wilcox, who twisted, seeking an excuse to ease himself from the conversation and avoid the involvement that so worried him.

"It's a language I enjoy," replied Kalenin. "Sometimes I listen to your B.B.C. Overseas broadcasts."

An unexpected confession, judged Snare. And one that could create problems for the man.

"They're very good," offered Snare, inadequately.

"Sometimes a little misguided and biased," returned Kalenin.

The reply a Russian should make, assessed Snare. Now there was no danger in the original remark.

Although a small man, the Russian looked remarkably fit, despite the rumoured dedication to work. Snare found him vaguely unsettling; Kalenin had the tendency to remain completely unmoving, using no physical or facial gestures in conversation. The man reminded Snare of a church-hall actor, reciting his responses word-perfect, mindless of their meaning.

"Excuse me," muttered Wilcox, indicating the British ambassador, who stood about ten feet away. "I think I'm needed."

Good man, judged Snare. He'd exonerate him from any criticism of the embassy when he returned to London. He saw the faintest frown ripple Kalenin's fare at the departure.

"There are other opportunities for practising the language, of course," said Snare, conscious of the time at his disposal.

"At receptions like this," suggested Kalenin, mildly.

"Or at trade gatherings, like those of Leipzig," said Snare. He had to hurry, risking rebuttal, he decided.

Kalenin was looking at him quite expressionlessly. It would never be possible to guess what the man was thinking, realised Snare. Debriefing him would take years; and a cleverer man than Charlie Muffin.

"In fact," continued the Englishman. "I think you met a colleague of mine recently at Leipzig."

"Wonder what they're talking about," said Braley, leaning against the far wall forty feet away.

"Our turn will come, if all goes well," said Cox, descending two inches from his calf exercise.

"I wish you'd stop doing that," protested Braley, breathily. "I find it irritating."

Cox looked at him, surprised.

"Sorry," he apologised. Sensitivity of a sick man confronted with good health, he rationalised. Poor guy.

Cox was a joke who needed replacing, decided Braley, enjoying his new intimacy with the C.I.A. Director. He'd get the man moved as soon as possible.

"A colleague?" Kalenin was questioning, accepting champagne from a passing tray. He didn't drink, Snare noted, holding his own glass untouched. Kalenin was a careful man, he decided, unlikely to make any mistakes.

"Yes. At the British tractor stand."

"Ah," said Kalenin, like someone remembering a chance encounter he had forgotten.

Taking the lead, he said: "Have you seen your friend lately?"

"No," said Snare, intently. "But I know fully of your conversation."

Kalenin had his head to one side, examining him curiously, Snare saw. His reply did not appear to be that which Kalenin had anticipated, he thought.

"My friend found the conversation most interesting," he tried to recover, momentarily unsettled.

"Did he?" responded Kalenin, unhelpfully.

Snare felt the perspiration pricking out and wanted to wipe his forehead. It would be wrong to produce a handkerchief, he knew, resisting the move. There could only be a few minutes left before an inevitable interruption and the damned man was making it very difficult.

Harrison had been *bloody* lucky.

"In fact," Snare went on, "he would very much like to continue it."

The curious look persisted.

"But that would be difficult, wouldn't it?" said Kalenin. He smiled for the first time, an on-off expression like someone following an etiquette manual that recommended a relaxed expression exactly five minutes after the first meeting.

"Difficult," agreed Snare. "But not impossible."

Kalenin frowned again, then shrugged. What did that mean? wondered Snare. Quickly he pulled his hand over his forehead; the sweat had begun to irritate his skin. Kalenin would have seen it, realising his nervousness, he thought, worriedly.

"Perhaps that's a matter of interpretation. And differing opinion," said Kalenin, obscurely.

Cuthbertson was right, thought Snare. There *were* to be conditions.

"I'm sure the difficulties could be resolved to the satisfaction of both interpretations," assured Snare.

Kalenin had probably survived for so long by being so cautious, decided the Briton. He felt happier at the new direction of their conversation.

"It would need the most detailed discussion."

"Of course," agreed Snare.

"And would probably involve expense."

Snare swallowed, nervously. The meeting *would* be as successful as Harrison's, he determined. Despite the outward calm, he guessed Kalenin was a desperately scared man.

"I don't see expenditure being a problem," said Snare.

"Not half a million dollars?" questioned the General, eyebrows raised.

Snare paused, momentarily. "Anything," Cuthbertson had said. "Anything at all."

"Certainly not half a million dollars," guaranteed Snare.

Kalenin smiled, a more genuine expression this time.

"Do you know the Neskuchny Sad, Mr. Snare?"

For a moment Snare didn't understand the question, then remembered the gardens bordering the Moskva River. He nodded.

"I've taken to walking there most Sundays," reported the Russian. "I feel it's important for an inactive man to get proper exercise."

"Indeed," concurred Snare, wondering the route towards which the Russian was guiding the conversation.

"I've made it a very regular habit. Usually about 11 A.M."

"I see," said Snare, relaxing further. It was almost too simple, he thought.

"I really am most anxious about my health," expanded Kalenin. "I'm quite an old man and old men believe that misfortune will befall them any day."

Wrong to relax, corrected Snare. There was a very real reason for this apparently aimless conversation.

"But that is often a groundless apprehension," he responded. "I've every reason to suppose that your health will remain good for a number of years."

"It really is most important that I *know* that," insisted Kalenin. "In fact, if I thought these Sunday constitutional walks were doing me more harm than good, I'd immediately suspend them."

"I think the walks are most beneficial. Certainly at this time of the year," said Snare.

From his left, the Briton detected Colonel Wilcox returning, conforming to their rehearsal. Snare turned to greet Cuthbertson's friend.

"We've been discussing health," threw out Kalenin, eyes upon Snare.

"Very important," said the attaché, unsure of the response expected.

"I've been telling Mr. Snare of exercises I've begun, to ensure I remain healthy for many years."

Wilcox hesitated, waiting for Snare's lead.

"And I've been assuring the General," helped the operative, "that continuing good health, into a very old age, has become a subject of growing interest in England."

Wilcox frowned, baffled by the ambiguity. What a stupid occupation espionage was, he decided. Silly buggers.

"Quite," he said, hopefully.

Kalenin looked across the room, to the rest of the Russian contingent.

"I must rejoin my colleagues," he apologised.

"I've enjoyed our meeting," said Snare.

"And so have I," said Kalenin. "And remember the importance of good health."

"I will," accepted Snare. "In fact, I might take up walking for the few remaining weeks I have in Moscow."

"Do that," encouraged Kalenin. "I can recommend it."

"Appeared to go well," said Braley, watching the two men part. "I'd just love to get my hands on Snare's report."

"We will," predicted Cox, stationary now. "When the British are forced to admit us, officially, we can demand the files already created."

"We've got to get in first," cautioned Braley.

Snare coded his report that night, determined it would exceed in detail and clarity Harrison's account from East Germany. It hadn't been difficult to prepare a better report, decided Snare, reading the file that had taken him three hours to complete. The evidence was incontestable now. When this operation was successfully concluded, he decided, Britain would be regarded as having the best espionage service in the Western world. He sealed the envelope, personally delivering it to the ambassador's office for the diplomatic pouch. And I will be known to be part of that service, he thought, happily. A vitally important part. He would keep the Sunday appointment with Kalenin, he decided, then return to London the following week; perhaps Cuthbertson would insist that he accompany him to the personal briefing of the Prime Minister.

As the weekend approached, Snare felt the euphoria of a man ending a prison sentence, ticking off the last days of his incarceration. Just eight more days and he would be back in London, he consoled himself: it would be a triumphant homecoming.

On the Thursday, he decided to buy souvenirs, assembling the currency coupons that would give him concessions in the foreign exchange shops. Some of the intricately painted dolls, he decided, preferably in national costumes.

He was arrested walking along Gorky Street, towards the G.U.M. department store. It was meticulously planned, taking little more than two minutes. The leading Zil pulled up five yards ahead, disgorging four men before it stopped and when he half turned,

instinctively, he saw the second car, immediately behind. Four men were already spread over the pavement, blocking any retreat.

To his back was the wall. And the gap between the
two cars was filled by both drivers, standing side-by-
side and completing the box.

"Please don't run," cautioned a man, from his right.
He spoke English.

"I won't," promised Snare. There was no fear in his
voice, he realised proudly.

"Good," said the spokesman and everyone seemed
to relax.

Charlie gazed around the lounge of his Dulwich home,
revolving the after-dinner brandy between his hands.

"You've made a good home, darling," he said.
There was an odd sound in his voice, almost like
nostalgia.

Edith smiled, a mixture of gratitude and apprehension. Her money had bought everything.

"I try very hard to please you, Charlie," she reminded.

He concentrated completely upon her, reaching over
and squeezing her hand.

"And you *do,* Edith. You know you do."

"I don't mind about affairs, Charlie," she blurted.

He remained silent.

"I'm just frightened it'll go wrong, I suppose."

"Edith," protested Charlie, easily. "Don't be silly.
How could that happen?"

"Love me, Charlie?"

"You know I do."

"Promise?"

"I promise."

"You're the only man I see colours with, Charlie,"
she said, desperately. "I wish to Christ I'd never inherited the bloody money to build a barrier between us."

"Don't be silly, Edith," he said. "There's no barrier."

The phone rang, a jagged sound.

"That girl from the office," said Edith, accusingly, holding the receiver towards him.

"Sorry to trouble you at home so late," said Janet, formally.

"What is it?" demanded Charlie, irritation obvious in his voice.

"You were to go directly to Wormwood Scrubs tomorrow?"

"Yes."

"Sir Henry wants that cancelled. You're to be at the office at nine o'clock. Sharp."

Very mliitary, mused Charlie; just like her godfather's parade ground.

"But that . . ." began Charlie.

"Nine o'clock," repeated the girl, peremptorily. "I've already informed the prison authorities you won't be coming."

"Thank you," said Charlie, but the telephone had been replaced, destroying the sarcasm.

"What is it?" asked Edith, as he put down the telephone.

"My meeting with Berenkov has been scrapped," reported Charlie. "I've got to see Sir Henry at 9:00 A.M."

"What does that mean?" asked the woman, worriedly.

"What I've argued for the past ten months," replied Charlie. "That you can't run the service like an army cadet corps. I told you they'd need me."

"Don't get too confident, will you, Charlie?"

"You know me better than that."

"It's just so bloody dangerous."

"It always has been," said Charlie, tritely.

10

It took Sir Henry Cuthberson an hour to explain the operation upon which they had been engaged for the past four months, culminating in Harrison's death and Snare's capture.

Charlie sat relaxed in the enormous office, aware of Wilberforce's eyes upon him, his face masked against any emotion. Several times the Director stopped during the account, but Charlie's complete lack of response kept forcing him into further details.

"That's it," completed Cuthbertson, at last. "The whole story."

Still Charlie said nothing.

"I was very wrong about you, Muffin," offered the Director, finally.

"Really?" prompted Charlie. Now I know how Gulliver felt among the little people of Lilliput, he fantasised. Edith's warning of the previous night presented itself and he subdued the conceit. It *would* be stupid to get too confident, as she had warned.

"Your debriefing of Berenkov has been brilliant, absolutely brilliant. I've written a special memorandum to the Minister, telling him so."

He must remember to question Janet about it, he thought. Cuthbertson was a lying sod.

"Thank you," said Charlie.

"And you were quite right about Berenkov having a contact at the research station at Portland. Naval intelligence got him a week ago."

"I'm glad," said Charlie. Berenkov would be upset at the cancelled visit, Charlie knew.

Silence descended in the room like a dust sheet in an empty house. Charlie gazed over Cuthbertson's shoulder, watching the minute hand on Big Ben slowly descend towards the half-hour position. It would be the size of four men, he guessed; maybe even bigger. It would be a noisy job, cleaning it, he decided. How Wilberforce, with his irrational dislike, would be hating this interview, he thought.

Cuthbertson looked at Wilberforce and Wilberforce returned the stare.

"I would like you to accept my apology," capitulated Cuthbertson.

"I was to be demoted," reminded Charlie. He'd let Cuthbertson get away with nothing, he determined.

"Another mistake," admitted the Director. "Of course there's no question of that now."

Because your balls are on a hook, completed Charlie, mentally.

"And some expenses ... ?" coaxed Charlie.

Cuthbertson stared directly at him. He really hates my guts, thought Charlie.

"Already reinstated," promised Cuthbertson.

Another query to put to Janet, thought Charlie. Wilberforce shifted. Was it embarrassment for his superior or irritation? wondered Charlie.

"I will accept that although they initially did well, I sent inexperienced men into the field on this latest operation," confessed Cuthbertson. He snapped his mouth shut after the sentence, like a man realising he was dribbling.

Never before in his life, Charlie knew, would Cuthbertson have been forced to make so many admissions of error. He would not be a man to forget such humiliation. His head pulled up, so that he was looking directly across his desk.

"So we need your help, Charles."

"Charlie," corrected the operative.

"What?"

"Charlie," he repeated, unrelentingly. "My friends call me Charlie."

Cuthbertson swallowed. The man would have enjoyed standing on one of those elevated platforms, watching over the Wall the body of the man he believed to be me burning beside the Volkswagen, Charlie decided. What, he wondered, had happened to the girl called Gretel?

"We need your help, Charlie," recited Cuthbertson, the words strained.

Charlie looked at him, allowing the surprise to show.

"How?" he asked.

Cuthbertson covered the exasperation by concentrating on the blank blotter before him. After several moments, he looked up again, under control.

"I want you to establish the link with Kalenin and bring him across," announced the Director.

It was a mocking laugh from Charlie, an amazed refusal to accept the words he was hearing.

"There is nothing—nothing at all—that is funny about what I've said," insisted Cuthbertson, tautlipped.

Impulsively, Charlie stood up, pacing around his chair.

"No," he agreed. "Nothing funny whatsoever . . ."

He stood behind the chair, hands resting on its high back, like a man at a lecture.

". . . It is just madness," completed Charlie. "Stark, raving madness . . ."

"I don't see . . ." tried Wilberforce, but Charlie refused the interruption.

"Please," he said. "Please, just listen to me. A year ago we broke a European spy ring, headed in this country by Alexei Berenkov . . ."

"For God's sake, forget the bloody man Berenkov," erupted Cuthbertson, releasing his anger. "He's got nothing to do with what we're discussing . . ."

"He's got *everything* to do with it," rebuked Charlie, emphatically. "Can't you see it, for Christ's sake?"

Cuthbertson winced, but said nothing; a court martial offence, judged Charlie.

"What do you mean?" asked Wilberforce, trying to buffer the feeling between the two men.

Ignoring Edith's warning of the previous night, Charlie burst on, "I'm astonished you can't see what's happening . . ."

The outburst had gained him the attention of both men, he saw. Cuthbertson would be worried he'd made the wrong assessment, like all the others.

"We destroyed their system . . . a system that had cost them time and money and which we now know was enormously important to them," elaborated Charlie. "Suddenly, from the shadows, appears General Kalenin, the genius of the K.G.B., a man no one has seen for two decades, asserting he wants to defect. With the same remarkable timing, there are stories in all the major communist publications that he's under pressure, giving the defection credence."

He stopped, looking to both men. Neither spoke.

"Like a rabbit coming out of a hat, he appears at Leipzig, exactly as he's indicated to Colonel Wilcox . . ."

Cuthbertson was doodling flowers on to his blotter and Wilberforce had begun mining his pipe: as a child, the second-in-command would have had a security blanket, Charlie decided.

". . . and, like simple innocents, we grab at it," took up Charlie. "We expose an operative, get fed a load of defection bullshit and then our man, who has identified himself, gets shot. As if this weren't warning enough, we go through the same procedure a month later in Russia and lose a second man."

They weren't accepting his arguments, Charlie realised.

"It's the oldest intelligence trick there is," Charlie insisted. "Make the bait big enough and so many fish will swarm you can catch them by hand."

Cuthbertson shook his head. "I can't agree . . . we've been unlucky, that's all. Others agree with me."

"Others?" jumped Charlie, immediately.

"The analysis section, upon which you place such reliance," said Cuthbertson, quickly.

There was more, Charlie knew, remaining silent.

"The initial approach was made at the American embassy," reminded Cuthbertson, reluctantly. "The C.I.A. assessed the media attacks on Kalenin and made the same decision as we did."

Charlie threw back his head, theatrically, braying his laughter.

"Oh, Jesus!" he said. "This is too much. Don't tell me the Americans are riding shotgun on the whole operation."

"They've sought involvement," conceded the Director. "But I'm keeping the whole project British; they can have access to the debriefing in the course of time."

Charlie made much of walking back around the chair and seating himself. Washington would be furious at being kept out, he knew.

"I am aware," he began, speaking very quietly and with control, "that I am badly regarded in this department, a reminder of a British intelligence system that made some very bad mistakes . . . mistakes that meant changes were almost inevitable . . ."

He hesitated. They were back with him now, he saw.

"But I have proved myself, if proof were needed, with the Berenkov debriefing," he continued. "I know espionage intimately . . . I'm an expert at it. You are a soldier, used to a different environment . . . a different set of rules . . ."

"What is the point you are trying to make?" broke in Cuthbertson, testily.

"That we're being set up," said Charlie, urgently. "A trap is being created and you are walking blindly into it . . ."

Again, Cuthbertson shook his head in refusal.

". . . Cut off now, before it's too late," pleaded Charlie. "A committed man like Kalenin wouldn't defect in a million years."

"You're scared," accused the Director, suddenly.

"You're damned right I'm scared," agreed Charlie, open in his irritation. "Two agents plucked off within days of encountering Kalenin! We should all be terrified. If he has his way, he'll wreck the whole bloody department."

"I want Kalenin," declared Cuthbertson, pedantically.

"But he isn't *coming*," insisted Charlie.

"He is," said the Director.

"Then tell me why Harrison and Snare have been hit," demanded Charlie.

"Because Kalenin is frightened."

Charlie frowned, genuinely confused. "What the hell does that mean?"

Cuthbertson paused at the impertinence, then dismissed it.

"On each occasion," enlarged the Director, "sufficient time elapsed for both men to dispatch full reports to London. Kalenin has allowed that, wanting the meetings to be relayed here. Both meetings were in public places . . . they would have been noted. And Kalenin would have known that. So he protected his back by going for them, once they'd served their purpose . . ."

He groped among the papers that leafed his desk.

". . . Snare refers several times to Kalenin's ill-concealed fear . . ."

". . . bloody right," said Charlie. "And I might concede your point if Snare had been killed too. But he's alive. By now, scientifically and without any pain, they will have taken apart the man's mind, right back to the age of two. Kalenin wouldn't have risked the inevitable exposure of his defection by letting Snare live, if the defection were genuine."

"They've promised us consular access in three weeks," rejected Cuthbertson, triumphantly. "They wouldn't do that if Snare wasn't perfectly fit and had been subjected to any torture, physical or mental . . ."

Charlie sat, waiting, opening and closing his hands.

"Rubbish," he said, at last. "They will have stripped him to the bone."

"The terms of your employment with the department do not allow you to refuse an assignment," reminded the Director.

"I know," said Charlie quietly.

"And I am ordering you to go."

Charlie knuckled his eyes, then looked up at the men who despised him. He sighed openly. He'd given them the chance to avoid making fools of themselves, he decided. Now it was entirely their fault.

"Did American intelligence know how Harrison and Snare were making contact?"

"Not that we know of," said Wilberforce.

Charlie sat, unconvinced. "Both meetings were at public functions," he said, talking almost to himself. "Washington would have known."

He looked up to Cuthbertson.

"They want involvement?" he queried.

"Desperately," agreed the Director.

"Give it to them," advised Charlie. "The payment stipulates dollars. Let the money be their entry."

"Why?" demanded Cuthbertson.

"To give me the opportunity for contact," said Charlie. "I don't want the Americans to have any idea that anyone is trying to pick up from Harrison or Snare. String them along by discussing money for a week, to give me time . . ."

"That won't work," warned Wilberforce, happy to have found a flaw. "Our embassy cover for you to go to Moscow doesn't come into operation for another three weeks."

"I'm not going to Moscow under your cover," lectured Charlie. Again he was reminded of Edith's warning about conceit, but discarded it.

". . . In the last three months you've arranged the crossing into Eastern Europe of two men whom you regarded highly," he said. "One is dead, the other is in Lubyanka. I'll get to Moscow myself."

"Don't be ridiculous, Charles," rebuffed Cuthbertson. "No one can enter Russia like that."

"Charlie," reminded the operative.

"Charlie," accepted the Director, tightly.

Charlie smiled, openly, so both men could see. He would have to be very careful not to go too far, he decided.

"Do you want the defection . . . if defection there is . . . to work?" asked Charlie.

"Yes," said the other man, instantly.

"Then I want to operate as I always have done."

"If it goes wrong," cautioned the Director, "then you'll be the sufferer."

"Sir Henry," accepted Charlie, smiling. "We both know why I'm being brought back into active service. And what will happen if I fail."

Cuthbertson did not answer the accusation.

"I'll need a large petty cash advance," stipulated Charlie. He'd take some good wine to Janet's flat that evening, he decided.

The Director nodded, defeated.

"I'll want to know what's happening all the time," said Cuthbertson, hopefully. "And I'll need receipts."

Charlie nodded.

"Of course," he agreed.

Cuthbertson waited, guessing there was more.

". . . And it would help to have my old office back," said Charlie. "If we're going to work on this, we'll need instant contact with each other . . ."

Cuthbertson nodded, his normally red face puce with emotion.

"I'm very worried about this," said Wilberforce, after Charlie had left.

"I'm terrified," confessed Cuthbertson. Why couldn't it have been Charlie Muffin shot in an East German ditch, he thought, regretfully. Even if he succeeded in this operation, decided the Director, he'd still ease him from the department, despite the promises he'd given. The man was quite insufferable.

The cherry trees were in full bloom, whitening the shrubbery outside Keys's office. Far away, people wandered ant-like into the Lincoln memorial, and in the park in front teenagers were clustered around an improvised guitar recital. It was very American and comforting, he thought.

"So how do you assess it?" demanded the Secretary of State, turning back into the room.

Ruttgers, who had arrived in Washington just one hour before and knew he would be affected by jet-lag very soon, shrugged, unwilling to commit himself.

"I don't really know," he said. "Kalenin has appeared, almost too easily. And from my last meeting with the British Director, it's obvious the man is discussing asylum."

"Do you believe it's genuine?"

"I don't know enough about it to make a judgment," avoided Ruttgers, easily.

"Do the British suspect why their operatives have been hit?"

"They haven't a clue," assured Ruttgers, confidently. "They think it's just K.G.B. surveillance and Kalenin being over-cautious."

"What about the request for money?"

"A stalling operation," guessed the C.I.A. chief. "They are trying to send someone else in."

"Will we be able to spot him?"

Ruttgers shifted, uncomfortable at the question. "I don't know," he replied, honestly. "I've got the Moscow embassy on full alert: the man will have to have some official cover, so we should be able to pick him up."

Knowing the Secretary of State's health fetish, Ruttgers never smoked in the man's presence. The need for a cigarette was growing by the minute.

It was time he came to the point of the meeting, decided the Director.

"The British are incredibly arrogant," he embarked. "It's about time they forgot they were ever a world power and realised how unimportant they've become these days."

"What do you mean?" demanded the Secretary of State, aware now that Ruttgers had a proposition.

"The President is due to tour Europe in November?"

Keys nodded.

"It would be a terrible snub if he visited every capital except London," predicted the C.I.A. chief.

"You've got to be joking," rebuked Keys. "I could never make a threat like that."

"You wouldn't have to," insisted Ruttgers. "Just to hint would be enough. Cuthbertson's a pompous old fool . . . he'd collapse the moment any ministerial pressure was put on him. And there would be pressure, without the need for an outright threat."

Keys shook his head, still doubtful.

"This could go badly wrong," he said.

"Or be the most overwhelming success," balanced Ruttgers.

"We'll provide the money?" guessed Keys.

"Oh yes," agreed Ruttgers. "I'm going to make it available. Once we're financially involved, we've got another lever to demand greater access."

"Keep a check on the money," said Keys. "Congress is almost insisting on petty cash vouchers these days."

Ruttgers looked pained.

"Of course we will," he guaranteed. "The numbers are being fed through the computer now. We'll have a trace on each note."

"I don't like this," repeated Keys, looking out over the gardens again. The police had begun to break up the guitar session, he saw. Why couldn't the kids have been allowed to continue? he wondered. They hadn't been causing any harm.

"It worries me," he added.

"It'll worry us more if the British get away with Kalenin by themselves," insisted Ruttgers.

"True," agreed Keys, sighing.

"Will you make the threat about cancelling the London visit?" asked the Director.

"I suppose so," said Keys, reluctantly.

Janet sat easily in the chair before her godfather, quite unembarrassed at his discovery of her affair with Charlie.

"But why, for God's sake?" pleaded the soldier. "You can have absolutely nothing in common."

Janet smiled, enjoying herself.

"At first," she explained, "he intrigued me . . . he was so different from any man I'd encountered before . . . more masculine, I suppose . . ."

She paused, preparing her shock.

". . . and actually," she went on, alert for the old man's reactions, "he's really quite remarkable in bed."

Cuthbertson's face went redder than normal and he gazed down at his desk to avoid her look.

"Do you love him?" he asked, still not looking at her.

"Of course not," said Janet, astonished at the question.

"Good," said the Director, coming back to her.

Janet frowned, waiting.

"I've involved him in the most vital operation in which he's ever been engaged . . ."

". . . The Russian thing that killed Harrison?"

Cuthbertson nodded, apprehensively, but his goddaughter showed no feeling.

"It is imperative that he succeeds," he said simply.

"Why are you telling me this?" demanded the girl.

"Because from this moment on I want to know everything that the man does during every minute of his existence. I've got him under constant surveillance . . . and I want to know your pillow talk as well."

Janet grinned at the expression: he must have got it from a women's magazine, she supposed, the sort they read in Cheltenham.

". . . ask him the odd question . . . he'll need to relax with someone . . . find out how he feels . . ."

Imperceptibly, he glanced at his watch. The electronic division would have completely bugged her flat by now, he estimated. Particularly the bedroom; some of what they heard would be unsettling, he thought, looking at the girl. Imagine, he recalled, he'd once held her in his arms in a baby's shawl!

"I know how he feels," reported Janet. She hesitated, then went on: "He resents your appointment . . . and the people you've brought in with you . . . the department is something to which he is deeply committed. Actually, I think it's the only thing for which he has any real feeling."

The Director sat nodding, accepting her assessment.

"So he'll do his best?"

"For the department . . . not for you."

Cuthbertson shrugged. "I still want to know how he feels about this assignment."

"You want me to spy on him?" asked the girl.

Cuthbertson nodded. "Will you do it?"

"I suppose so," she agreed, after a few seconds. "It all seems a bit daft, really."

"Good girl," praised Cuthbertson. "Oh," he suddenly remembered, "two more things."

The girl sat, waiting.

"Get those expenses back that I cut," he instructed. "I'm restoring them. And take a note for the Minister . . ." He paused, assembling his words, then dictated the memorandum of praise for Charlie Muffin's handling of the Berenkov affair. He had the girl read it back, then said: "One final paragraph."

"In fact," he dictated, "Charlie Muffin was one of my most able and eager workers in the very difficult capture of Alexei Berenkov, which I initiated and headed."

He smiled across the desk. "That'll do," he dismissed, contentedly.

"What you're asking me to do is in the nature of an assignment, isn't it?" asked Janet, remaining seated.

"Yes," he agreed, curiously.

"So there'll be some expenses, won't there? Good expenses?"

He paused, momentarily.

"Yes," he accepted, sadly. "There'll be liberal expenses."

Later, after she'd typed the memorandum, Janet sat back in her chair in the outer office and smiled down at her lover's name.

"Everyone in the world is trying to screw you, Charlie Muffin," she said, softly.

"Poor Charlie," she added.

11

In other circumstances, decided Charlie, as the coach left Sheremetyevo airport and picked up the Moscow road, he'd have enjoyed the experience. Perhaps he and Edith would be able to take one of the weekend holidays, some time. Then again, perhaps not.

His method of getting to Moscow had been simple and he was confident that neither Cuthbertson nor the C.I.A., who surrounded their activities with mystique and confusion, would realise how it had been done.

He'd simply gone to the Soviet authorised travel agency in South London, knowing they issued the In-tourist coupons for Russian vacations, and bought him-self a £56 weekend package tour to the Russian capital.

The visa had taken a week and he'd had a pleasant flight out with a clerk from Maidenhead on his first trip abroad ("I read in a travel magazine that you need bath plugs; you can borrow mine if you like") and fif-teen members of a ladies' luncheon club from Chelmsford fervently anxious to experience romance without actual seduction ("there's such excitement about forbidden places, don't you think?").

By now Cuthbertson would have discovered he'd left England, decided Charlie, gazing out at the Soviet woodland.

The observation in London had been rather obvious and easy to evade. He glanced at his watch: the men outside the Dulwich house, which he'd left under a clearly visible pile of cleaning in the Porsche driven by

Edith, would probably still be assuring Cuthbertson he hadn't left.

Would Cuthbertson approach Edith directly? he wondered. Unlikely, decided Charlie. But if the Director *did* summon his wife, Charlie was confident Edith would have no difficulty convincing the former soldier that when she had left on her cleaning expedition, Charlie had been inside the house. Edith had always found it easy to lie, he thought, reflectively.

Which was different from Janet, he thought. Her sudden interest in the operation ("I know what happened to Harrison; isn't it natural I should worry about you?") had amused him. Poor Janet, he thought. He wondered what incentive Cuthbertson had offered. Money, probably. She was a greedy girl.

The coach crossed the river and then pulled along the Moskva embankment towards the Rossiya hotel. Charlie disembarked as instructed by the officious Intourist guide and stood patiently for thirty-five minutes to be allocated a room, assuring the Maidenhead clerk when he finally collected his key, that he wouldn't forget the bath-plug offer.

There was still twenty-four hours before Kalenin was supposed to appear in Neskuchny Sad, so Charlie continued to be the tourist, prompt for the regimented mealtimes, always waiting for the coaches taking them in their pre-paid tours, diligent in his purchases of souvenirs. He'd surprise Janet, he decided, by taking her Beluga caviar.

I should feel nervous, he thought, during the interminable wait for dinner on Saturday night. Almost immediately, he corrected the thought. Not yet. So far there was nothing about which to be apprehensive. But there would be, soon, he knew. Then he would need the control of which he had always been so confident.

He was able to avoid the Sunday morning tour with less difficulty than he had expected, placating the Russian woman with the promise that he would be ready for the Basil Church and Lenin's tomb in the afternoon, then happily watching the Maidenhead clerk depart in close conversation with the secretary of the ladies' luncheon club who appeared likely to admit access to forbidden places.

"To work," Charlie told himself, stepping out on to the embankment. He touched his jacket, in needless reassurance: the pocket recorder that he had checked and rewound lay snugly against his hip, quite comfortably.

It would be a long walk, he realised, striding out towards the Karmeni Bridge. But it would be safer to travel on foot, he knew. It was a fine, clear morning and he found the exercise stimulating; if it all goes wrong, he thought, wryly, then the only exercise he would know for the rest of his life would be the sort that Berenkov was getting in Wormwood Scrubs.

In the middle of the bridge spanning the Moskva, he rested, gazing over the parapet at the island in the middle, apparently an aimless tourist with time to waste. After fifteen minutes, he determined he was not being followed and continued his walk, turning down towards the Alexandre Palace.

It was 10:45 A.M. when he entered the park. A standing man is conspicuous, according to the instruction manual, he reminded himself. He meandered along the pathway leading towards the river, pacing the journey, turning back in perfect time to the entrance. The walk had reassured him. The park was not under obvious observation, he decided. His close survey didn't preclude watching and listening points immediately outside, of course.

Kalenin entered exactly on time, a short, chunky figure in an overcoat too long for him and a trilby hat that seemed to fit oddly upon his head. The General hesitated, then began strolling along the same path that Charlie had taken a few minutes earlier, gazing curiously from side to side, a man hopeful of an appointment.

The Englishman watched him go, making no effort to follow. It was ten minutes before Charlie accepted

Kalenin was free from close surveillance and another ten minutes before he located the man again.

The General had stopped walking, sitting on a seat halfway down one of the longest paths, the uncomfortable hat alongside him on the bench. The man was so short his feet scarcely touched the ground, Charlie saw, as he approached. It was difficult to believe he was one of the most feared and powerful men in Russia.

General Kalenin turned to him, his eyes sweeping Charlie's westernised clothes and appearance as he smiled, very slightly.

Charlie gave no response, but sat the far end of the bench, stretching in the pale sun. It would be too cold to sit there very long, he decided. He hoped Kalenin didn't engage in the ambiguity he'd shown Snare and Harrison. There was little reason why he should.

"A wise man always breaks his exercise by sensible rest periods," opened Charlie.

"Yes," agreed Kalenin.

Both spoke without looking at each other.

"This is my fourth Sunday here," complained Kalenin. "I was beginning to think Snare had missed the point during our conversation at the embassy."

"How is he?" asked Charlie. Snare wouldn't have enquired after his well-being had the situation been reversed, Charlie reflected. He was glad Kalenin was going to avoid nuance and innuendo.

"Perfectly all right," assured the Russian.

"There'll be a suspicion if he's not accused or released soon," warned Charlie.

"I know," agreed Kalenin, looking along the bench for the first time. "I want to get it over with as soon as possible."

"How soon?"

"Three weeks?"

Charlie looked back at the Russian, frowning.

"That's very short," he protested.

"But very possible," argued Kalenin. "There has been arranged for months that I should make a visit to Czechoslovakia . . ."

". . . So the crossing would be into Austria . . . ?"

Kalenin nodded. "Difficult?" he queried.

"I don't think so," said Charlie. "We've got a pretty strong system there."

"So it would suit you?"

"Yes. I think it would be perfect."

Kalenin shivered, conscious of the cold.

"The Americans are deeply involved," announced the General, unexpectedly.

Charlie was suddenly attentive.

"What do you mean?"

"They identified both Snare and Harrison to our people . . . I had to act . . ."

Charlie laughed, surprised.

"The bastards," he judged mildly.

"If Harrison hadn't run, our people wouldn't have shot him. They're trained to react that way."

"I know," accepted the Briton, remembering Checkpoint Charlie. "Why do people always run?"

"Lack of experience," recorded Kalenin, sadly. "And neither he nor Snare were very good. It would have been difficult for them to have avoided suspicion."

The same assessment that Berenkov had made, recalled Charlie. He was glad he had the tape recorder.

"Why would Washington do it?" probed Charlie, still conscious of the recording.

"Involvement," said Kalenin, looking surprised at Charlie's question. "They don't know of you, do they?"

"I hope not."

"They suspect somebody is here, though," said the General. "They've alerted their embassy staff."

The K.G.B. would have an excellent monitoring system on the American embassy, Charlie knew. He supposed Washington would be aware of it: it would have been safer for them to have sent the instructions in the diplomatic bag. The mistake showed a lack of planning, decided Charlie. Or panic.

"Have they listed the name of Charles Muffin?" asked the Briton. He'd had to register in the hotel under his real identity and knew it would take little more than a day to check the hotels on the Intourist list.

"No," reassured the General. "They just know somebody is coming."

So Cuthbertson was keeping him anonymous to the Americans. Thank God.

"Who's working on the request?" asked Charlie.

"The new C.I.A. station chief is a man called Cox," identified Kalenin. "A sportsman . . . runs around the embassy."

"We won't meet again," stipulated Charlie, protectively. He was leaving the following night and knew that unless he monitored Kalenin's movements, which was virtually impossible, Cox could never discover his presence in the capital. If there *were* a confrontation, he'd kill the man. It would be necessary for his own protection: and Cox's organisation had been responsible for a British operative's death, which would give the killing some justification in Cuthbertson's view.

"There'll be no need," said Kalenin. He was silent for several moments. Then he asked, "Will Washington provide the money?"

"On the promise of participation, I would expect so," responded Charlie. "If they won't, Whitehall will . . ." he smiled. ". . . they're extraordinarily keen to get you across."

Kalenin grinned back.

"It feels strange to be so important."

"You never had any doubts, did you?" asked Charlie.

Kalenin shrugged. "I was concerned the request wouldn't have been taken seriously."

Charlie thought back to the last dispute with the Director and Cuthbertson's insistence that the defection was genuine. The little man was very convincing, thought Charlie. But then security men were often excellent actors.

The Briton became conscious that Kalenin was studying him minutely.

"You're recording this meeting?" the Russian demanded, expectantly.

"Whitehall will need some proof, other than my word."

"Of course," accepted Kalenin. "But it would be awkward if the tape were found at the airport."

"It won't be," promised Charlie.

"Just in case, I'd better guarantee the flight," cautioned Kalenin.

Momentarily Charlie hesitated, then gave the flight number of the aircraft in which he was leaving Moscow on the Monday night. It was getting very cold and there was still a lot to discuss, Charlie realised.

"Shall we walk?" invited Kalenin and Charlie stood, gratefully, falling into step beside the Russian. The man couldn't be more than five feet tall, thought Charlie. Maybe less.

"The Americans will mark the dollar notes," warned the Russian.

"I expect so," agreed Charlie.

"So the money will be worthless."

"Yes," agreed Charlie.

"That won't do," protested Kalenin.

"I can ask for it in advance of the cross-over and 'wash' it," offered Charlie.

"It's important to do so."

"I know that," said Charlie.

"I'll need to know that it's been done."

They turned on to a bisecting path.

"What date do you have in mind?"

"The nineteenth," said Kalenin. "That will give me a week in Prague."

"We'll need to meet again," said Charlie.

"You'll have to be careful of the Americans," continued Kalenin. "They might leak it to the *Statni Tajna Bezpecnost* and the involvement of the Czech secret police could be embarrassing."

"I'll think of something," promised Charlie. After today's meeting there could be protection in American presence, he decided.

They walked in silence for several minutes.

"Alexei Berenkov is probably my best friend," Kalenin announced, suddenly.

"Yes," prompted Charlie.

"How is he adapting to prison?"

"Badly," said Charlie, honestly.

"He would," agreed Kalenin. "He's not a man to be caged."

Kalenin would have adjusted fairly easily, assessed Charlie. The General was a man who lived completely within himself.

"Poor Alexei," said the Russian.

Again there was silence.

"Do you think there'll be any serious problems?" demanded Kalenin, suddenly, stopping on the pathway to reinforce the question and looking intently up at the Briton.

Charlie answered the look.

"I don't know," he replied. "Are you frightened?"

Kalenin considered the question, hands deep inside the pockets of his overlarge coat. He was right to feel uncomfortable in that hat, decided Charlie; he looked ridiculous.

"Yes," replied the General, finally, "I'm a planner, not a field operative like you. So I'm very scared. I'm under intense pressure from a man in the Praesidium. That's why I want it all over so quickly."

"Being a field operative doesn't help," offered Charlie. "I'm nervous too. I always am."

The smaller man stood examining him for several moments.

"The other two men wouldn't have admitted that, Mr. Muffin," he complimented. "I'd heard you're very sensible."

It came as no surprise to learn the K.G.B. had a file upon him.

"I'm a survivor," agreed Charlie.

"Aren't we all?"

"We'll know the answer to that on the nineteenth," said Charlie.

They stopped inside the park gate, hidden by shrubbery.

"If the crossing is to be on the nineteenth, then I will be in Prague by the thirteenth," undertook Charlie.

"It should be a casual encounter, like that of today," advised Kalenin.

"Do you know the Charles Bridge?"

The Russian nodded.

"Let it be at midday on the fourteenth, on the side looking away from Hradčany Castle towards the sluices."

Kalenin nodded, but stayed on the pathway, looking downwards. His shoes were brightly polished, Charlie saw.

"The Americans frighten me," said Kalenin.

Charlie waited, frowning.

"I could arrange quite easily for you to have a minder," offered the Russian.

Charlie laughed, genuinely amused.

"A British operative guarded by the K.G.B.?" he queried. "Oh, come on!"

"It could be done without suspicion," insisted Kalenin.

Such detailed surveillance would pad the file already existing upon him in Dzerzhinsky Square, he realised. The awareness alarmed him.

"I prefer to work completely alone," reminded Charlie. "I always have."

"As you wish," said Kalenin. "But sometimes that's not possible."

So I'm to be watched, realised Charlie. In Kalenin's position, able to invent any reason for such observation, he would have taken the same precautions, he knew. The irony amused him. It would soon need a small bus to accommodate the number of people assigned to him.

"Until the thirteenth," said Kalenin, offering his hand.

"Yes," agreed Charlie.

"Isn't that number considered unlucky in your country?" asked the Russian, suddenly.

"I'm not superstitious," rejected Charlie.

"No," said Kalenin. "But I am."

Charlie arrived back at the hotel in time for the afternoon tour, content with the morning's encounter. He was very alert, conscious of everyone around him, but was unable to identify anybody who could obviously have been an American paying special attention to his party.

When he attempted to run his bath that night, he discovered the plug missing. Smiling, he crossed the corridor and paused outside the clerk's doorway, listening before knocking. The noise they were making, thought Charlie as he turned away, was quite astonishing. But then, some girls were inclined to shout a lot. At the top of the corridor, he saw one of the women concierges who occupy a desk on every floor of Russian hotels. She had a pen in her hand and a book was open before her. She was staring fixedly towards the sounds.

"My friend suffers from catarrh," said Charlie, smiling.

The woman looked expressionlessly at him, then began writing.

"Miserable sod," judged Charlie, going back to his own room and jamming the bath with a wad of toilet paper.

"I have been asked," said Cuthbertson, stiffly, "to make this operation a joint one between our two services."

"Yes," said Ruttgers, happily. He looked appreciatively around the Whitehall office: the British knew how to live, he thought. All the furniture was genuine antique.

"It might not be easy," protested the Briton.

Ruttgers spread his hands, expansively.

"Not a matter for us, surely?" he said, soothingly.

"We merely have to obey the instructions from our superiors."

Cuthbertson sat staring at him, saying nothing. The left eye flickered its irritation and Ruttgers looked down at the cigarette in his hand: just like Keys, he thought. There was a hostility in the man beyond that which the American had expected from being told to co-operate.

"I'm sure it will work fine," said Ruttgers, briskly. "Now what I want to do is send in one of my men to make contact with Kalenin. You haven't had much success so far, after all."

From Moscow that morning he'd been assured that no new operatives had been posted to the British Embassy. Now was the time to make demands, when they were unsure of themselves.

"I'm afraid things have progressed beyond that point," said Cuthbertson, smirking.

Ruttgers waited, apprehensively.

"We have made very successful contact with Kalenin and arranged a crossing," continued Cuthbertson, condescendingly. "There really is very little that we will need you for."

Ruttgers flushed, furiously. Braley had been right, he thought. Cox was an incompetent idiot to have placed him in this position. He'd order the withdrawal immediately.

"It's a ministerial order that we co-operate," reminded Ruttgers. He was confused, trying to recover his composure.

"I wonder," mused Cuthbertson, completely sure of himself, "if that order would have been issued had the Cabinet had the opportunity to listen to what Kalenin had to tell my man in Moscow."

"What?" demanded the C.I.A. Director, nervously.

"I know how Harrison and Snare were detected, Mr. Ruttgers," said the Briton.

"It's a lie," snapped the American, instinctively.

"What?" pounced Cuthbertson.

Ruttgers fidgeted, annoyed with himself.

"Any allegation about my service," he insisted, inadequately.

"I'm accepting your presence, under protest, because it's an order," said Cuthbertson, in his familiar monotone. "I'm making the transcript available to the Cabinet, together with my feelings about it. But make no mistake, Mr. Ruttgers. The part you and your service play in this matter will be a very subservient one."

The matryoshkas dolls, the rotund, Russian figures that fit one in the other, making a family of eight, were displayed on the dressing-table, reflected into the bedroom by the mirror. She'd liked the caviar, too, thought Charlie.

Janet lay, damp with perspiration, against his chest, nudging him with her tongue. He'd have to do it again in a minute, he knew. He really was getting too old.

"Sir Henry is very impressed," she said.

"So he should be."

"But I gather he and Wilberforce are annoyed you made the trip without their knowing."

"Too bad."

"What's Kalenin like?"

"Little bloke. Frightened, but he doesn't show it."

"Half a million is a lot of money."

"But worth it," insisted Charlie. What would she do for half a million, wondered Charlie, stroking her hair.

She pulled away from him and wedged herself upon one arm.

"Do you think it will work, Charlie?"

"It's got to," replied the man.

"For whom?" she demanded. "You. Or the department?"

"Both," said Charlie, immediately. "It's equally important for both."

"They're only using you, darling," warned Janet, stretching back again. "They'll fuck you in the end if it serves the purpose."

"Yes," agreed Charlie, softly. "That's the worrying thought."

12

The distrust was tangible, a positive obstruction between them, thought Charlie, sitting comfortably in the Director's office.

He'd created the situation and was contented with it, examining the reactions like a researcher studying slides beneath a microscope.

Wilberforce was in his accustomed chair, examining his peculiar hands as if seeing their oddness for the first time, and Cuthbertson was attempting to improve the design on an already tattooed blotter. He regretted now his earlier agreement to the Moscow tape recording being played in full, guessed Charlie.

Ruttgers stood by the window, driven there by the anger that had pulled him from the chair as the Neskuchny Sad recording had echoed in the lofty room. The American Director was swirled in a cloud of tobacco smoke.

Braley perched in the stiff, uncomfortable chair, pumping at his inhaler.

"I repeat what I have already told Sir Henry," protested Ruttgers, staring out into Parliament Square. "Kalenin, if indeed the voice we have heard is that of Kalenin, is lying."

"To what purpose?" enquired Charlie, in apparent innocence.

"What right have you got to question me?" demanded the American, imperiously.

"The right of a man whose two colleagues have already perished as a result of C.I.A. involvement and whose neck is currently on the block," retorted Charlie.

Ruttgers looked at Cuthbertson for rebuke, but when none came reiterated, "The C.I.A. did not inform upon your operatives."

"Then what can it mean?" coaxed Charlie. This encounter couldn't have gone better, he thought.

"That he was lying," said Ruttgers, without thought. "Or that it isn't really Kalenin."

"Do you really feel that?" seized Cuthbertson, ahead of Charlie, but prompting for different reasons.

"It's a reasonable assumption," said the American.

"Then it's an equally reasonable assumption that the whole episode is phoney—as I have argued for many weeks now. And that we should stop this thing now without any more risk to either service or any more people," said Charlie.

Ruttgers stayed at the window, recognising the alley into which he had been backed.

The cracking of Wilberforce's knuckles came over the sound of Braley's wheezing; it was like being a sick visitor in a terminal ward, thought Charlie.

"It *must* be pursued to the end," asserted Ruttgers, finally.

Cuthbertson looked up from his defaced blotter.

"By my service," he qualified.

Ruttgers said nothing.

"And on my terms," stipulated the ex-soldier.

Ruttgers sighed, accepting he had no bargaining counters. He nodded, briefly.

"On our terms," demanded the British Director, insistent on a commitment.

"Agreed," confirmed the American, tightly.

"Which means I want somebody . . ." Charlie paused, looking at the asthmatic Braley, ". . . him, with me in Czechoslovakia. At all times, in fact . . ."

Cuthbertson and Wilberforce looked up, frowning curiously.

"Because having a C.I.A. man with me guarantees I

won't be exposed by them, doesn't it?" smiled Charlie, looking between the two Americans for reaction.

Ruttgers turned away from the window, his face clearing.

". . . But that's . . ."

". . . me setting *you* up," interrupted Charlie. "I want him with me, but taking as little part as I determine in the discussions I have. He's just always got to be within ten yards."

"Ten yards?" queried Braley, the inhaler held loosely in his hand, like a blackboard pointer.

"From that range, I'm classified as an expert shot," said Charlie, simply. "I'd see an arrest coming, long before ten yards . . ."

He stared directly at Ruttgers.

". . . I shall draw a gun from the British embassy," he recorded. "And before any arrest, I'll kill your man. And that would create an embarrassing international *cause célèbre,* wouldn't it?"

"This is preposterous!" complained the American, going to Cuthbertson.

"Yes," agreed the British Director, "it is, isn't it? But after the misfortunes that have occurred so far, I can see Muffin's point of view."

"You want constant involvement," contributed Wilberforce. "This is surely what's being proposed?"

Another blocked alley, saw Ruttgers.

"I want to make it quite clear," began Ruttgers, formally, "that a full account of this meeting will be sent to the Secretary of State, Willard Keys, for whatever use he might see fit to make of it in his discussions with the President about the forthcoming European visit. I'm sure he'll find it sad that the special relationship between our two countries has reached such a point."

"I'm sure he will," picked up Cuthbertson, unafraid. "I hope his distress will be matched by that of the British cabinet when they have had the opportunity fully to study the transcript of the Kalenin conversation."

This was very bad, realised Ruttgers. If the British pressed the point, Keys would abandon him, assuring the President he had no knowledge of the entrapment of Snare and Harrison. He could be brought down by this débâcle, realised the American.

"I think we are allowing stupid, unwarranted animosity to cloud the point of this meeting," he attempted.

"Which is to bring successfully to the West the most important Russian defector since 1945?" lured Charlie.

Ruttgers nodded, suspiciously.

"To a scenario which you don't accept?" said Braley, to help his superior.

"Doesn't it seem to you that, Harrison and Snare apart, the whole thing has gone just a little too easily?" asked Charlie.

"Yes," agreed Ruttgers, immediately. "But then again, how else could it have gone? Kalenin is in a unique position to manipulate circumstances to his own advantage and to behave in a manner that others would find impossible."

"So now you accept it's genuine?" said Wilberforce, head sunk deeply on his chest so that the words were difficult to hear.

"I'm saying we . . . ." Ruttgers paused, remembering the rebuke, ". . . you," he corrected, "should make the Prague meeting."

"Have your analysts examined every report and transcript?" asked Charlie.

"Yes," said Braley, shortly.

"To what conclusion?" demanded Charlie.

"Apprehension," accepted Ruttgers. "But not the outright doubt that you're expressing, Charles."

"Charlie," stopped the Englishman.

Ruttgers frowned. "What the hell are you talking about?" demanded the American Director.

"If you must use it, the Christian name is Charlie," he corrected.

Ruttgers looked in bewildered exasperation at Cuthbertson, who shrugged. Muffin was amazingly vindictive, decided Cuthbertson. Almost childishly so.

"It just doesn't feel right," swept on Charlie, enjoying his control of the meeting. They were all uncomfortable and confused, he saw, happily.

"I know what you mean," said the American, staring at the peculiar Englishman. "But at this stage, we've got no choice but to go along with it."

"What about access to Snare?" reminded Charlie, coming back to Cuthbertson.

"Deferred," reported the permanently red-faced man. "Without any explanation."

Charlie shook his head, unhappily, as if the delay confirmed his concern.

"We can do nothing except follow Kalenin's lead," stressed Braley, again taking his chief's lead.

"I believe Kalenin when he said he's putting me under surveillance," said Charlie, opening a new course of discussion. "Even here, in London."

Both Ruttgers and Cuthbertson frowned.

"Have you been aware of it?" asked Wilberforce.

"No," said Charlie. "But if they were good, and they will be, then I wouldn't know of it, would I?"

"So?" queried Ruttgers. He examined the Englishman with interest. He was a complete professional, thought the C.I.A. Director: the only one, apart from himself and Braley, in the room.

"So we *must* wash the money."

Ruttgers moved, uncomfortably, like a subordinate aware of an indiscretion in front of the managing director at a firm's Christmas party.

"Now wait a minute . . ."

". . . we can't wait a minute," cut off Charlie. "If that money isn't broke down, Kalenin will know about it. You heard the tape. He just won't cross."

"What'll that involve?" asked Braley.

"To do it sufficiently publicly?" said Charlie, rhetorically. "I'd say about two weeks to cover London, the South of France and Austria. And that's not allowing for any unforeseen difficulties."

"We *did* record the numbers," confessed Ruttgers. "And it took us nearly a week, even feeding into a computer."

"We'll still be able to keep a check," said Charlie.

"How?" asked Ruttgers.

"Knowing every number is the optimum. And unnecessary," Charlie lectured. "To trace the money, if you need to, we'd need just a sample. Braley and I could use a pocket calculator and feed in a section of the cleaned money."

Ruttgers frowned, doubtfully.

"And let's face it, you're being incredibly cautious," stressed Charlie. "At a conservative estimate, it'll take two years completely to debrief Kalenin. And even then he'll need and probably demand help with a new identity, place to live and permanent guards. We'll be aware of his location for ten to fifteen years from now. The money is very unimportant, except to him."

And to Congress, thought Ruttgers. But the Briton was talking complete common sense. It really didn't matter and Keys would have to accept that ground conditions made the change necessary. Equated against the amount of money the C.I.A. spent yearly, sometimes on madcap projects, this investment was infinitesimal, anyway. Ruttgers nodded acceptance, shifting from the window.

The man found it difficult to remain in any one position, thought Charlie, watching Ruttgers settle into the chair he had already quit four times during the course of the meeting.

Like Charlie, Ruttgers felt there was something indefinably wrong about the whole thing. But he did have what he wanted, a man involved from this moment in every aspect of the crossing, he reassured himself.

"Right," he accepted. "We'll do what you suggest and hope it's right."

"That's the trouble," seized Charlie. "None of us knows whether we're right or not. And we won't for three weeks."

Berenkov looked a caricature of the man he had once been, thought Charlie. The Russian edged almost apprehensively into the room, all exuberance gone, standing just inside the door and staring at his visitor, awaiting permission to advance further.

The man's skin looked oily, but flaking, as if he were suffering from some kind of dermatitis, and there was a curtain of disinterest over his eyes. He shuffled rather than walked, scarcely lifting his feet, and when he spoke it was in the prison fashion, his lips unmoving.

"Good of you to come, Charlie," he said. The voice was flat, completely devoid of expression.

"You don't look good, Alexei."

The man stayed where he was, just inside the entrance.

"Come in, Alexei. Sit down," invited Charlie. He felt patronising.

"It's been over a year," mumbled Berenkov, through those unmoving lips, disordering his hair with a nervous hand as he settled at the table. "One year, three months and two weeks."

And two days, knew Charlie. How long, he wondered, before men with a sentence as long as Berenkov's stopped marking the calendar?

He had nothing to say, realised Charlie.

"I brought some magazines," he tried, hopefully. "They're being examined by the prison authorities, but it'll only take a few minutes. You should have them by tonight."

"Thank you," said Berenkov, unresponsively.

He wouldn't read them, Charlie realised. The degree of apathy into which the Russian had sunk would mean he spent all his cell-time staring at the wall, his mind empty. Berenkov had the smell of cheap soap and the proximity of too many bodies, thought Charlie, distastefully.

"Any tobacco?" cadged the Russian, hopefully.

Charlie pushed some cigarettes across the table. Berenkov took one, hesitated, then slid the rest into his pocket. He stopped, frozen for a second to await the challenge from Charlie. The Briton said nothing and Berenkov relaxed.

"Doing anything interesting?" asked the Russian.

Charlie looked at him curiously. It was a question without hidden point, he decided.

"No," he generalised. "Just clerking."

Berenkov nodded. He'd barely assimilated the words, Charlie saw.

"But I'm going away on holiday for a few weeks," covered Charlie. "I won't be able to see you for a while."

Momentarily the curtain lifted and Berenkov frowned, like a child being deprived without reason of a Sunday treat.

"You won't abandon me, Charlie?" he pleaded.

"Of course I won't," assured Charlie, holding without any self-consciousness the hand that Berenkov thrust forward. "I made you a promise, didn't I?"

"Don't let me down, Charlie. Please don't let me down."

In Janet's flat, three hours later, he swilled brandy round the bowl, watching it cling to the side. He looked up suddenly at the girl.

"You know what?" he demanded.

"What?" responded Janet.

"Berenkov was right. All those months ago."

"About what?"

"Me and imprisonment. He said I wouldn't be able to stand it and he was right. I'd collapse even before he has."

"So what would you do?" asked the girl, seriously.

"If I knew capture was inevitable," asserted Charlie, "then I'd kill myself."

She was going to cry, realised Janet. Shit, she thought.

Kalenin began setting out the tanks for Rommel's assault upon Tobruk and then stopped the displacement, half completed. He wouldn't play tonight, he decided.

He straightened, staring down at the models. The forth-coming Czech visit and what was to follow made it unlikely that he would recreate the battle for some weeks.

If ever. The thought came suddenly, worrying him. Why, he wondered, was Kastanazy being so implacable in his campaign? It was an over-commitment in the circumstances and therefore stupid, likely to cause him problems. And Kastanazy wasn't usually a stupid man.

Kalenin shrugged, replacing the tanks into their boxes. Perhaps it was time Kastanazy was taught a lesson, he thought, sighing. The man wasn't liked in the Praesidium, Kalenin knew.

The General went into the regimented living-room, carefully positioned the cover over the headrest of the easy chair and sat down, looking with satisfaction round the apartment, enjoying its clinical neatness. Not one thing out of place, he thought. He smiled at the thought. The words that could sum up his life, he decided: everything in the right place at the right time.

He rose abruptly, without direction, bored with the inactivity. The next month was going to be difficult to endure, he realised.

He poured a goblet of Georgian wine, then stood examining it. Berenkov had been disparaging about his country's products, recalled Kalenin. "Bordeaux has much more body. And a better nose," his friend had lectured, during their last meeting.

He envied Berenkov, Kalenin suddenly realised. The man was all he had ever wanted to be. But Berenkov had been caught, Kalenin rationalised. Which made him fallible.

Will I be detected? wondered Kalenin, finishing his wine.

13

A large map table had been brought into Cuthbertson's office and several two-inch ordnance sheets pinned out in sequence showing the Czech border with Austria, with all the routings into the capital. Beside the maps were boxes of blue and green flags, awaiting insertion.

It was an exercise that Cuthbertson understood and he moved round the table assuredly, aided by Ruttgers, who had returned that morning from Washington and from a meeting with both Keys and the President. The C.I.A. Director was pleased the President was involved; it elevated the operation to exactly the sort of status he considered necessary.

"By the thirteenth, we'll have moved over a hundred men into Austria," recorded Ruttgers. "And we're airlifting in sufficient electronic equipment to guarantee a complete radio link-up between every operative."

Cuthbertson nodded. The previous day there had been a full Cabinet meeting which he had attended and he knew that afterwards there had been direct telephone calls between the Prime Minister and the American leader.

"We're matching that commitment," he confirmed. "Man for man."

The resentment at the American involvement still rankled with him: the Cabinet hadn't shown sufficient outrage, he thought, critically.

Cuthbertson stared fixedly at Ruttgers, then at the map table.

"Your cigarette is smouldering," he complained. "Can't you extinguish it?"

"Once Kalenin crosses that border," said Ruttgers, casually stubbing the offensive butt and looking down at the map, "the net will be so tight that a fly couldn't escape."

"I'm still a little concerned about Austria," said Wilberforce, "we can't mount an operation of this size without them learning about it."

"We can and we will," bullied Ruttgers, immediately. "By the time they discover anything, it'll be all over."

"It still seems diplomatically discourteous," protested the tall man.

"That's not the way they'll see it," guaranteed the C.I.A. chief. "Austria is the bridge between East and West, don't forget. They'd be scared shitless knowing in advance someone of Kalenin's importance was going to move through their territory. Sure they'll bleat and complain at the United Nations and both our governments will dutifully apologise at the intrusion. But privately Austria will be damned glad we kept them out so their relations with Moscow don't suffer."

Cuthbertson smiled patronisingly at Wilberforce, indicating he shared the American's assessment.

"It'll be difficult to make all our displacements until we know when and how Kalenin intends crossing. But we can bottle up the city."

He paused, looking at Ruttgers.

"You sure your house is safe?"

"For Christ's sake," said Ruttgers, "the C.I.A. have owned it for twenty years . . ."

". . . which means the K.G.B. probably know about it," intruded Wilberforce.

"Not this one," promised Ruttgers, who regarded it as vitally important that Kalenin should be lodged instantly at an American-owned property. He was growing increasingly confident he could elbow the British aside once Kalenin had defected.

"Do you think I'd run the risk if I wasn't a hundred per cent certain?" he added.

Cuthbertson nodded, accepting the assurance. He took a gold flag indicating Kalenin from a third box and inserted it into the marked house on Wipplinger-strasse.

"Anyway," pointed out the British Director, "he won't be there longer than an hour. It will just be somewhere to stop, change his clothes and then leave for the airport."

"You've fixed that?" queried the American.

Cuthbertson, who had already entered another gold marker in Schwechat, nodded.

"We've officially informed the Austrians we want to shift embassy furniture and equipment over a three-week period. There will be four dummy flights, moving things round for no reason except to get them used to it."

As he talked, Cuthbertson was flagging the area round the house where Kalenin would be held. He worked on a grid pattern, marking down from the Danube Canal, bordered by the post office and Aspern Square across the old city hall and Am Hof Square and embracing the Hofburg Palace, the Spanish Riding School and running up to Volksgarten. Blue flags indicated concealed observations; green designated open surveillance, on foot or in cars.

"That's a hell of an area," remarked Ruttgers, echoing Wilberforce's thoughts.

"But necessary," insisted Cuthbertson. "This outline covers the situation for a concealed, unpursued crossing . . ."

He opened a drawer and took out some red-headed pins.

". . . I think there should be a contingency situation for an emergency flight, possibly under pursuit . . ."

He held up the crimson markers.

". . . and we won't be able to insert these, showing it, until Muffin's meeting on the thirteenth from which I hope to know the crossing point."

"Then what?" queried Ruttgers.

Cuthbertson sighed.

"I hope it doesn't happen," he said. "But in case it does, we'll want a back-up team at the crossing spot. If the Russians learn it's Kalenin, they'll come across without bothering whose country they're violating. I'll have a transfer car waiting, into which we can put Kalenin . . ."

He hesitated at the American's frown.

"I'll only need three minutes at the outside," he said. "If the Russians chase, I want them to be able to locate almost immediately the crossing car, which will take off to loop Vienna and apparently make for the Italian border . . ."

"While the real car completes the journey to the airport?" accurately guessed Ruttgers.

"There's a lot wrong with that," argued Wilberforce. The two Directors stood, waiting.

"What do you imagine the Austrian authorities are going to do while all this is happening?" criticised the civil servant.

"As much as possible," said Cuthbertson, confidently. "All I want is the transfer. The Austrians will be chasing the car that crossed and which the Russians or Czechs followed. Not one of my operatives—or an American—will be involved, apart from the initial holding operation. From then on, Austrian police pursuit is exactly the sort of diversion I want."

"What about the driver of Kalenin's original car?" probed Wilberforce, obstinately.

"He'll have to be sacrificed," said Cuthbertson, easily. "I want an explosive device fitted, during the transfer. To detonate within five minutes."

"So who will be driving?" asked Wilberforce.

"I had thought of Muffin," said Cuthbertson.

"He's too valuable: he'll have to travel on with Kalenin," protested Ruttgers.

"You're right, of course," accepted the British Director. "It'll have to be somebody else."

"There's Cox, currently attached to our Moscow embassy," offered Ruttgers, remembering his annoyance at the man's inability to detect Charlie's entry into Russia. "His involvement would be very natural. And he speaks Russian, which gives added validity for his secondment."

"All right," agreed Cuthbertson, carelessly. "Let's use him."

Wilberforce stood studying both men, wondering if either was really medically sane. He supposed the sacrifice of one life was justified, but he would have expected some distaste from those making the decisions: Ruttgers and Cuthbertson appeared almost to be enjoying it.

"Our debriefing team will be arriving in London next week," reported Ruttgers, avoiding looking directly at Cuthbertson.

"Yes," said the ex-soldier. He still hoped to persuade the Cabinet to retract permission for the interviews with Kalenin to be Anglo-American.

"We've got houses available here?" asked Ruttgers.

"Four," replied Cuthbertson. "Each is as secure as the other. They're all in the Home Counties."

"We'd like to examine them first," said Ruttgers.

The clerk-like American had been born out of his time, decided Wilberforce. He would have enjoyed bear-baiting or cock-fighting, watching animals gradually tearing themselves to pieces.

"A pointless precaution," defended Cuthbertson, holding his temper. "I will not have that sort of interference."

Ruttgers smiled. "I'd still like to be satisfied," he said.

"I'll raise it at the Cabinet meeting," undertook Cuthbertson, trying to avoid the commitment. "They might object, too."

"They won't," predicted Ruttgers. "But if you need authority," he continued, "go ahead."

Ruttgers was an easy man to dislike, thought Wilberforce.

"There's one other thing," said the American.

Cuthbertson concentrated upon his map positions, appearing disinterested.

"I thought one of us should go to Vienna personally to meet him."

Cuthbertson frowned, off-balanced by the suggestion.

"We'll *both* go," insisted the Briton, anticipating what Ruttgers was going to say and determined not to be upstaged by the other man.

"It's an American house," protested Ruttgers, who had wanted the opportunity to begin his persuasion upon the Russian.

"But a joint operation," reminded the former soldier, definitely.

Ruttgers nodded in curt agreement. He'd blown it, he decided, annoyed at himself.

Charlie Muffin relaxed happily in his former office, with space in which to move and its pleasant view of Whitehall. Like a child who has had its ball returned from a neighbour's garden, he smiled at Braley. He liked the man, he decided. Braley was a professional, which always gained his esteem: little else did, reflected Charlie.

They had finished the public laundering of the money the previous night, one day before each departed for Prague under embassy cover. The debriefing with Ruttgers and Cuthbertson had been easy and almost perfunctory, both Directors preoccupied with their pinned and flagged series of maps.

There had not, anyway, been any reason for a lengthy meeting, remembered Charlie. The operation had gone perfectly and had been identical in the casinos of Vienna, Monte Carlo, Nice and the Clermont and National Sporting Clubs in London.

Each night for the previous two-and-a-half weeks they had entered the high game rooms and changed fifty thousand dollars into gambling chips. After three hours mingling with the gamblers but never playing, they returned to the *caisse*, changed the chips back into unmarked currency and left the casino. The mornings of each day had been spent taking sample records, Charlie selecting notes at random and dictating their numbers to Braley, who had operated the pocket recorder.

The American was bent over it now, making the final calculation.

"According to my figures, we have a trace on fifty-five thousand dollars. That's twenty thousand in sterling, fifteen in French francs and twenty thousand in Austrian Schillings."

"Sufficient," judged Charlie, dismissively.

"It was very necessary though, wasn't it?" he added.

Braley nodded, positively. In Vienna, Braley had identified two known K.G.B. operatives, and Charlie had located a third in Monte Carlo. For that number to have been seen meant the surveillance on Charlie had been absolute, they had decided at their meeting with the Directors.

"At least Kalenin knows we're following his stipulations to the letter," said Braley.

"He knows exactly what we're doing," agreed Charlie. "What bothers me is that I haven't a clue about him."

"Still apprehensive?" queried Braley.

Charlie nodded. "Very," he admitted.

The man's nervousness was unsettling, thought the American. He wondered how the Englishman would behave if things went wrong in Czechoslovakia.

14

Charlie spent the day before his Prague flight in Rye. He had telephoned from London, so when he arrived at the station, Wilkins, who had been manservant and chauffeur to Sir Archibald throughout his directorship of the department and retired on reduced pension rather than work for another man, was there to meet him.

They had known each other for twenty years, but Wilkins greeted him formally, allowing just the briefest, almost embarrassed handshake, before opening the car door.

It was a magnificent Silver Shadow, maintained by a chauffeur who adored it in a condition of first-day newness.

"Car looks as good as ever," complimented Charlie.

"Thank you, sir," said Wilkins, steering it from the parking space.

"If ever Sir Archibald fires you, come and drive for me," invited Charlie, attempting what had once been a familiar joke between them.

"Thank you, sir," replied Wilkins. He'd forgotten, thought Charlie, sadly. The response should have disparaged a Ford Anglia, a troublesome vehicle that Charlie had once owned.

"Sir Archibald was sorry he couldn't come to the station," recorded Wilkins.

"Isn't he well?"

"He's waiting at the house," avoided the chauffeur.

"Isn't he well?" repeated Charlie, but Wilkins didn't reply and after several minutes Charlie relaxed against the shining leather, knowing the conversation was over.

No, thought Charlie, as he hesitantly entered the lounge of Sir Archibald's home, darkened by drawn curtains against the summer brightness. Sir Archibald wasn't well. It was incredible, Charlie thought, remembering his last meeting in Wormwood Scrubs with Berenkov, how quickly people collapsed. The former Cambridge cricket blue who had captained his county until his fiftieth birthday and who, three years before, had been an upright six-foot-three who could command attention by a look, was now a bowed, hollowed-out figure, with rheumy eyes and a palsied shake in his left hand. He'd developed the habit of twitching his head in a curious, sideways motion, like a bird pecking at garden crumbs, apprehensive of attack, and he blinked, rapidly and constantly, as if there were a permanent need for clear vision.

"Charlie!" he greeted. "It's good to see you."

The blinking increased. He was very wet-eyed, Charlie saw.

"And you, sir," replied Charlie. Odd, he thought, how instinctive it was to accord Sir Archibald the respect he found so difficult with Cuthbertson.

"Sit down, lad, sit down. We'll drink a little whisky. I've some excellent Islay malt."

Charlie had already detected it on the old man's breath. Sir Archibald filled two cut-glass goblets, raised his and said: "To you, Charlie. And to the department."

"Cheers," said Charlie, embarrassed. It had been a forced toast and he wished the old man hadn't made it.

Sir Archibald sat in a facing chair and Charlie tried to avoid looking at the shaking hand. The old man had always detested physical weakness, remembered Charlie. During his tenure as Director, medical examinations had been obligatory every three months.

"Been unwell," complained Sir Archibald, confirming the expected irritation at his own infirmity. "Caught flu, then pneumonia. Spent too much time in the garden on the damned roses. Lovely blooms, though. Have to see them before you go."

"Yes," agreed Charlie. "I'd like that."

Sir Archibald drank noisily, sucking the whisky through his teeth. Charlie became conscious of the stains on his jacket and trousers and sighed. Sir Archibald was a very shabby, neglected old man, he thought.

"Good of you to come at last," said the former Director, floating the criticism.

"Been busy," apologised Charlie, inadequately.

Sir Archibald nodded, accepting the excuse.

"Course you have, course you have. See from the newspapers that you finally got Berenkov."

"Yes," conceded Charlie, modestly. "It was all very successful."

Sir Archibald added whisky to both their glasses, looking cheerfully over the rim of the decanter.

"Got a commendation, too, I shouldn't wonder? Your job after all."

"No," said Charlie, staring down into the pale liquid. "I didn't get a commendation. Two other operatives did though. Names of Harrison and Snare. You wouldn't know them; they arrived after you left."

"Oh," said Sir Archibald, glass untouched on his knee. The old man knew it would be improper to ask the question, Charlie realised, but the curiosity would be bunched inside him.

"It's very different, now, sir," said Charlie, briefly.

"Well, it had to be, didn't it?" offered Sir Archibald, generously.

"For two unpredictable, entirely coincidental bits of bad luck?" refuted Charlie, suddenly overcome by sadness at the figure sitting before him. "I don't think so."

"Come now, Charlie," lectured his old boss. "There had to be a shake-up and you know it."

"It hasn't achieved much."

"It got Berenkov," pointed out Sir Archibald.

"*I* got Berenkov, operating a plan evolved by you

and Elliot before the changes were made," contradicted Charlie.

"It was sad about Elliot," reflected Sir Archibald, reminded of his former assistant and trying to defuse Charlie's growing outrage. "I visit the grave sometimes. Put a few roses on it and ensure the verger is keeping it tidy. Feel it's the least I can do."

"I've never been," confessed Charlie, suddenly embarrassed. "I was in East Germany when the funeral took place."

"Yes, I remember," said Sir Archibald. "Not important. It's the living that matter, not the dead."

It had been one of Sir Archibald's favourite remarks, remembered Charlie.

"Yes," he agreed, shielding his goblet from another addition from his persistent host.

"Is it going to be difficult, Charlie?" demanded Sir Archibald, suddenly.

"What?" frowned Charlie.

"Oh, I know you can't give me details . . . wouldn't expect it. But is the operation you're involved in going to be difficult?"

Charlie smiled, nodding his head at his former chief's insight.

"Very," he confirmed. "The most difficult yet."

"Thought it was," said the old man. "Knew there had to be some reason for the visit."

Quickly he raised his shaky hand, to withdraw any offence.

"Appreciate it," Sir Archibald insisted. "Consider it an honour to be thought of like this, by you."

"It'll probably go off perfectly," tried Charlie, cheerfully.

"If you believed that, you wouldn't have bothered to come here to say goodbye," responded the former Director.

Charlie said nothing.

"Anything I can possibly do to help?" offered the old man, hopefully.

"No," thanked Charlie. "Nothing."

"Ah," accepted Sir Archibald. "So you could die?"

"Easily," agreed Charlie. "Or be caught."

Charlie paused, remembered Berenkov. "I'm not sure of which I'm more frightened, death or a long imprisonment," he added.

Sir Archibald gazed around the room. "No, Charlie," he agreed. "I don't know, either. But the risk isn't new: it's been there on every job upon which you've ever been engaged."

"This one is different," insisted Charlie.

The decanter was empty and Sir Archibald took another bottle from beneath the cabinet. They were regimented in lines, Charlie saw, before the door was closed. The former Director fumbled with the bottle, finally giving it to Charlie to open for him.

"Have the department handled it right?" demanded Sir Archibald, definitely. He was getting very drunk, Charlie saw.

"Competently," he said.

"But I'd have done better?" prompted the old man, eager for the compliment.

"I think you'd have had more answers by now," said Charlie. It wasn't an exaggeration, he thought. Sir Archibald could always pick his way through deceit with the care of a tightrope-walker performing without a net.

Sir Archibald smiled, head dropped forward on to his chest.

"Thank you, Charlie," he said, gratefully. It was becoming difficult to understand him.

"For coming," the old man added. "And for the compliment."

"I meant it," insisted Charlie.

Sir Archibald nodded. The glass was lopsided in his hand, spilling occasionally on to his already smeared trousers.

"Be very careful, Charlie," he said.

"I will, sir."

"Remember the first rule—always secure an escape route," cautioned Sir Archibald.

The training that got me back alive from East Germany, recollected Charlie.

"Of course."

Sir Archibald hadn't heard him, Charlie realised. His head had gone fully forward against his chest and he had begun to snore in noisy, bubbling sounds. Carefully Charlie reached forward and extracted the goblet from the slack fingers and put it carefully on to a side table.

He stood for several minutes, gazing down at the collapsed figure. Every day would end like this, he realised; it was another form of imprisonment, like that of Berenkov.

"Goodbye, sir," said Charlie, quietly, not wanting to rouse the man. He snored on, oblivious.

Wilkins was standing outside the room, waiting for him to leave.

"He's gone to sleep," said Charlie.

Wilkins nodded.

"He's not been well, sir," reminded the chauffeur.

"No," accepted Charlie.

"He misses the department . . . misses it terribly," said Wilkins in what Charlie accepted was the nearest the man had ever come to an indiscretion.

"And we miss him," assured Charlie. "Tell him that, will you?"

"Yes, sir," promised Wilkins. "It would please him to be told that."

The man turned to the hall table.

"He wanted you to have these sir," said Wilkins, offering him a huge bunch of Queen Elizabeth roses. "He's very proud of them."

"Tell him I was very grateful."

"Perhaps we'll see you again, sir," said Wilkins, knowing it was unlikely.

"I hope so," said Charlie, politely, knowing he would not make a return visit.

"What lovely flowers," enthused Janet, as Charlie handed her the roses three hours later.

"I got them from Sir Archibald Willoughby," reported Charlie.

The girl looked sharply at him.

"The Director wouldn't like it if he knew you'd seen him," said Janet, formally.

"Fuck the Director, he'll know anyway because his watchers followed me, all the time. They were so bloody obvious they should have worn signs around their necks."

"It's still improper," insisted the girl.

"If he doesn't like it, he can go to Prague tomorrow and put his head in the noose, instead of staying behind in a comfortable office sticking pins in maps."

The First Secretary, Vladimir Zemskov, was being cautious, judged Kalenin, unwilling to be openly critical before the full Praesidium.

"It is distasteful to us to have to demand an explanation from such an experienced officer as yourself, Comrade General," he said.

Kalenin nodded, appreciatively.

"But Comrade Kastanazy has made the complaint about the progress so far," hardened the Soviet leader. He waited, pointedly. "And the consensus of opinion," he continued, "is that insufficient thought and planning has been put into proposals to repatriate General Berenkov . . ."

"I refute that," said Kalenin, bravely.

Several members of the Praesidium frowned at the apparent impertinence.

". . . I asked to be given a certain period of time," reminded Kalenin. "I understood from Comrade Kastanazy that I was being allowed that time. To my reckoning, it has yet to expire . . ."

". . . There are only a few more days," reminded Zemskov. The man was offended, Kalenin saw, and the ambivalent attitude was disappearing in favour of

Kastanazy. They'd all follow Zemskov's lead, he knew.

"Allow me those days," pleaded Kalenin.

"But no more," said Zemskov, curtly.

I won't need any more, thought Kalenin.

15

Charlie invariably grew nostalgic about the East European capitals he visited, trying to envisage the life of centuries before and those years free of concerted oppression when the people delighted in grandiose architecture and extravagant monuments to their own conceit.

"Prague would have been a women's city," he told himself, in the taxi negotiating its way over the Manesuv Bridge. He stared along the Vlatva river towards the Charles Bridge upon which he was scheduled to meet Kalenin the following day.

"Please God, make it be all right," he mumbled. He became aware of the driver's attention in the rear-view mirror and stopped the personal conversation. A psychiatrist would find a worrying reason for the habit, Charlie knew.

The car began to go along Letenska and Charlie gazed up at Hradčany Castle on the hill. The remains of King Wenceslaus were reported to be there, he remembered. He should try to visit the cathedral before he left.

The reception at the embassy was stiffly formal, which Charlie had expected. It was an embassy unlike most others, in which he had no friends, and he guessed no one there would make it easy. The high-priority message from Downing Street to the ambassador would have indicated the importance of Charlie's mission, but equally it would have alerted the diplomat to the risk of having his embassy and himself exposed in an international incident that could retard for years the man's progress through the Foreign Office. It was right they should resent his intrusion, he accepted.

"I hope to leave within days," Charlie assured the First Secretary, who gave him dinner. Charlie's cover came from the Treasury, checking internal embassy accounts. It was the easiest way for quick entry and exit.

"Good," said the diplomat, whose name was Collins. He was a balding, precise man who cut his food with the delicacy of a surgeon. His attitude reflected that of the ambassador, Charlie guessed.

"There really shouldn't be any trouble," tried Charlie.

"We sincerely hope not," said Collins immediately.

He was regarded with the distaste of a sewage worker come to clear blocked drains with his bare hands, decided Charlie. Fuck them.

"There is one thing," said Charlie, remembering the threat made when the C.I.A. presence had been forced upon the department. It seemed rather theatrical now, but it was a precaution he would have to take.

"What's that?"

"I shall want a gun."

Collins looked at him, incredulously.

"A what?" he echoed.

"Don't be bloody stupid, man," replied Charlie sharply. "A gun. And don't say the embassy haven't got one because I had three sent out in the diplomatic pouch a fortnight ago."

Collins dissected his meat, refusing to look at him.

"The instructions to the embassy were signed personally by the Prime Minister," threatened Charlie, irritated by the treatment. He was behaving just like Ruttgers, Charlie thought, worriedly.

"I'll ask the ambassador," undertook Collins.

"*Tell* the ambassador," instructed Charlie. His anger was ridiculous, he accepted, quite different from his normal behaviour in an overseas embassy. Because of it, the meal became stifled and unfriendly and Charlie drank too much wine. He did it knowingly, anticipating the pain of the following day but needing it to submerge his fear and spurred by irritability. Twice during the dinner, offended at the continued pomposity of the First Secretary, Charlie stopped just short of fermenting a pointless dispute.

He retired immediately after the meal, sitting in the window of the room with a tumbler of duty-free whisky, gazing out over the darkened city. A thousand miles away, he ruminated, an old man for whom he would once have happily died was probably sitting in a window holding a larger amount of whisky, staring out over his rose bushes. The degeneration of Sir Archibald had frightened him, accepted Charlie. He snorted, drunkenly, at the thought. And Berenkov had frightened him and the assignment frightened him.

"Wonder I'm not constantly pissing myself," he mumbled.

Spittle and whisky dribbled down his chin and he didn't bother to wipe it.

"Got to stop talking to myself," he said.

He slept badly, rarely losing complete consciousness and always aware of himself through spasmodic, irrational dreams in which first Ruttgers and then Sir Archibald pursued him wielding secateurs and he panted to evade them, burdened by the wheezing Braley slung across his shoulders.

He abandoned the pretence of sleep at dawn, sitting at the window again, watching the sun feel its way over the ochre, picture-painted buildings in the old part of the city immediately below him.

He had the hangover he had expected. His head bulged with pain that extended down to his neck and his mouth was arid. It had been a stupid thing to have done and would affect his meeting with the Russian, he thought.

He breakfasted alone, in his room, uncontacted by anyone. Finally he approached Collins's office, determined to control the annoyance.

"The ambassador has approved the issuing of a revolver," said the meticulous diplomat.

"Yes," said Charlie. He felt too ill to compete with the man, anyway.

The weapon lay on the desk and Collins looked at it but refrained from touching it, as if it were contaminated. Charlie picked it up and placed it in the rear waistband of his trousers, at the small of his back, where it would be undetectable to anyone brushing casually against him and not be a visible bulge unless he fastened his jacket.

He was conscious of Collins studying him, critically.

"I don't bloody like it, either," said Charlie, venting his apprehension.

It was a warm, soft day and if he hadn't felt so unwell Charlie would have enjoyed the walk down the sloping, sometimes cobbled, streets.

The Charles Bridge is one of the ten that cross the Vltava to link both sides of the city but is restricted entirely to pedestrians. Each parapet is sectioned by huge statues of saints.

Charlie approached early from the direction of Hradčany, so he loitered before the shops in the narrow, rising approach to the bridge, stopping for several moments apparently to study the fading, pastel-coloured religious painting adorning the outside of the house at the immediate commencement. He was not being followed, he decided.

The bright sunlight hurt his eyes, increasing the discomfort of the headache. He felt sick and kept belching.

Slowly he began to cross the bridge, professionally glad it had been chosen as a meeting place. It was thronged with tourists and provided excellent cover.

He saw the American first.

Braley had approached from the opposite side of the river and had halted by one of the statues. He was wearing sports clothes and an open shirt, with a camera slung around his neck. It was very clever, conceded Charlie, reminded again of the fat man's expertise. Without creating the slightest suspicion, the

American was ideally placed to photograph the meeting between him and Kalenin.

So thick was the midday crowd he almost missed the General. The tiny Russian was standing where they had arranged, wearing a summer Russian raincoat that was predictably too long, staring up towards the sluices. Charlie felt a shudder of fear go through him and he shivered, as if he were cold. He gripped his hands tightly by his side, pushing his knuckles into his thighs.

"Too late to be frightened, Charlie," he told himself. "You're committed."

As he covered the last few yards, he tried to isolate the watchers in addition to Braley but failed. It was to be expected, rationalised Charlie. Those immediately around the K.G.B. chief would be the absolute best: Ruttgers and Cuthbertson would have people there as well, he knew.

Charlie grinned, despite the nervousness and discomfort. There hadn't been a moment for the past three months when he hadn't been under collective surveillance from one service or another, he thought. Presidents didn't get better protection.

He positioned himself alongside the Russian without looking directly at him.

"Sorry I'm late," he apologised. He was still dehydrated from the alcohol and his voice croaked.

"Not at all," assured Kalenin. "I was early."

Charlie felt the other man examining him.

"Are you all right?" asked the General. "You don't look well."

Charlie turned towards him.

"Fine," he lied.

Kalenin nodded, doubtfully.

"I'm afraid Snare has had a collapse," announced the General.

Charlie stayed, waiting.

"Apparently couldn't stand solitary confinement," reported the Russian. "Our psychiatrists are quite worried."

"He's in the Serbsky Institute?" predicted Charlie.

"Yes," agreed Kalenin. "It's remarkably well equipped."

"So we've heard in the West from various dissidents who've been brainwashed there," responded Charlie, sarcastically.

Kalenin frowned at the remark, then shrugged.

"My people will be upset at the news," said Charlie.

"It was quite unintentional, I assure you," replied Kalenin. "In the circumstances, I couldn't let him come into contact with anyone, could I?"

"No," accepted Charlie. "I don't suppose you could."

Kalenin looked back up the river.

"I've always liked Prague," he said, conversationally. "I think of it as a gentle city."

Charlie was perspiring, not just from the heat, and the pain in his head drummed in time with his heartbeat.

"We're not here to admire the city," he reminded, curtly.

Again Kalenin turned to him.

"Are you *sure* you're all right?"

"Of course."

"You're recording this meeting?" queried Kalenin, expectantly.

"Yes," said Charlie, patting his pocket. Kalenin nodded.

"You were very punctilious about the money."

Further along the bridge, Charlie saw Braley manœuvre for a photograph.

"I see your companion in Vienna and France is a little further along," continued Kalenin, without turning round. "Shall I meet him?"

The Russian was smiling, happy at his control of the situation.

"That's a matter for you," said Charlie, disconcerted.

"I think we should, in a moment," replied Kalenin. "I've worked out the crossing with great care and I don't want anything to go wrong: it's best he hears at the same time as you."

"We've also done a fair amount of planning," guaranteed Charlie.

Kalenin nodded again. He's patronising me, thought Charlie.

"The money will be in Austria?" demanded Kalenin.

"I've already lodged it at the embassy," said Charlie.

"Good," praised Kalenin. "Good. You really do seem to have put some thought into it."

The General turned, looking towards the American.

"To avoid repetition, shall we join Mr. Braley now?"

It would have been relatively easy to compare pictures taken in Austria and France against those of former personnel at the Moscow Embassy, supposed Charlie.

The American saw them approaching and moved against the parapet, gazing fixedly at the view.

"Are there many pictures of our meeting, Mr. Braley?"

Braley's chest pumped uncertainly.

"We were photographed as well as seen during the money-changing," enlightened Charlie, feeling sorry for the C.I.A. man.

Braley swallowed, trying to curb the nervous reaction.

"Good day, sir," he said to the Russian, awkwardly.

It sounded a ridiculous greeting in the circumstances and Charlie wanted to laugh. Nerves, he thought.

Kalenin continued walking, without replying, leading them from the bridge. He appeared very confident, thought Charlie; too confident, even. The man could ruin the whole thing by conceit, thought the Englishman, worriedly.

"There's a very attractive horologe in the old town," lectured Kalenin, like a tourist guide, as they reached the covered pavement. "And some pleasant cafés."

Charlie and Braley exchanged looks, but said nothing. The American was as uncertain as he was, saw Charlie.

Kalenin made a point of showing them the gilded timepiece before courteously seating them at a pavement table and ordering drinks. He and Braley had beer, but Charlie selected coffee.

"I have been thinking very deeply about what is to happen," said Kalenin slowly. He was speaking, thought Charlie, as Cuthbertson would have addressed a class at staff college.

Kalenin looked directly at both before continuing.

"I have become increasingly aware of the enormous value I have in the West," said the General. "Upon reflection a value far in excess of $500,000."

Braley moved to speak, anticipating a change of mind in the Russian, but Kalenin raised his hand imperiously, stopping the interruption. From somewhere in the square, Charlie knew, there would be cameras recording every moment of the encounter: the admiration of the horologe and selection of the conveniently free café table was very rehearsed.

"I am determined to be properly treated," continued Kalenin.

He was ill at ease with pomposity, thought Charlie.

"I don't think you need have any doubt about that," assured the Briton.

Kalenin looked at him, irritably.

"Allow me to finish," he demanded. "As I have already indicated, I will cross over on the nineteenth. I've arranged a visit to the border area in such a way as to allay any suspicion. I have selected Jaroslavice as the crossing point . . ."

The General paused.

". . . don't forget that," he instructed.

". . . Jaroslavice isn't on the border," corrected Charlie, immediately.

Kalenin sighed. "I know," he accepted. "I mention the town for map reference. I shall cross at Laa an der Thaya. I presume you will have people back at Stronsdorf, but that won't be enough . . ."

Charlie smiled at the man's behaviour. It wasn't natural, he knew. But Kalenin was sustaining it well.

"We won't forget the crossing point," he promised.

Kalenin looked at him sharply, suspecting mockery.

"I've not the slightest intention of crossing in the vague expectation of a reception committee in Stronsdorf," announced the General. "I must know the arrangements that have been made to receive me in the West. And be assured they will be followed."

Braley looked questioningly at Charlie, who nodded.

"You were quite right, sir," began the American at last, "in your assessment of your importance. If it will convince you of our awareness of it, let me say that both the British and American Directors are personally making the trip to Austria to greet you . . ."

Kalenin beamed.

"Exactly," he said, apparently not surprised by the news. "That's at exactly the sort of level I want to conduct the whole affair."

Charlie began to feel better and waved for more drinks, ordering a beer for himself this time. He stared around the square, trying to identify the watchers. It was hopeless, he decided, abandoning the search.

"What time do you intend to be at Laa?" he asked the Russian.

"Night will be best," said Kalenin, immediately. "According to my estimate, if we travel through Ernstbrunn and Korneuburg, we can reach Vienna in little over an hour . . ."

Charlie nodded, doubtfully. Longer, he would have thought.

". . . I want you waiting on the Austrian side of the border promptly at 10:30. But not before. I don't want a caravan of cars attracting attention," ordered Kalenin.

"It'll hardly be dark," complained Braley.

"Dark enough," insisted Kalenin.

"Shouldn't we arrange a contingency situation, in case there is any cause for your being delayed?" asked Charlie.

Kalenin smiled sympathetically at the Englishman.

"Instructing me on trade-craft?" he mocked.

"Trying to guarantee a successful operation, General," retorted Charlie, tightly.

"Nothing will go wrong," said Kalenin, confidently. "Nothing at all."

He raised his glass, theatrically.

"To a perfect operation," he toasted.

Feeling uncomfortable, both Charlie and Braley drank.

"And another thing," said Kalenin. "I want the money brought to the border. I want to see it . . ."

". . . But . . ." Charlie began.

". . . I want to see it," cut off Kalenin, definitely.

He stared at Charlie, alert for any challenge.

Charlie shrugged. "As you wish," he said.

"I *wish*," picked up Kalenin. "And please inform your people . . ." he paused, ". . . on both sides of the Atlantic," he qualified, "of my insistence at being accorded the proper reception and continued treatment befitting my position."

"We'll inform them," undertook Charlie. It would be interesting to see the reaction of both Directors when the tape was played in London, he thought.

"There need be no further contact between us," said Kalenin, curtly. "You know the crossing point and my demands . . ." he hesitated, looking at Charlie. ". . . be at Laa," he instructed the Englishman. "I shall remain in Czechoslovakia until I'm personally sure you hold the money and the Directors are somewhere in the capital."

Charlie nodded, frowning.

"You want me to make another crossing into communist territory?" he asked.

"Yes," smiled Kalenin, easily. "What possible apprehension need you have? It'll only be a few yards."

Abruptly the tiny Russian stood up.

"I will leave you," he said. He turned, then came back to them.

"Until the nineteenth," he said.

Charlie and Braley watched the tiny figure bustle

across the square and disappear along one of the covered pavements.

Braley extended his examination of the square, like Charlie aware they had been placed by design at the particular café table. They paid, rose and without talking, suspicious that listening devices might have been installed, walked into the open.

"Well?" demanded Charlie, as they slowly followed the route the General had taken. Both walked with their heads bent forward, so it would have been impossible for the conversation to have been lip read by their observers.

"It's wrong," judged Braley. "We've been set up."

"That's what I'm afraid of."

"Incidentally," side-tracked Braley. "That gun was visible when you sat down."

Charlie loosened his jacket, annoyed at the criticism. He hadn't checked its concealment by sitting down; a stupid mistake.

"Did you mean it, Charlie?" asked Braley, interested. "If there had been any C.I.A. involvement during the meeting, would you have shot me?"

"Yes," said Charlie, immediately.

Braley paused, then shook his head slightly. It was impossible to discern whether the attitude was one of disbelief or incredulity.

The C.I.A. man jerked his head in the direction in which Kalenin had disappeared.

"What do you think he's going to do?"

Charlie slowed in the shadow of the covered pavement.

"I wish to Christ I knew. I've tried every possible permutation and it still doesn't come out right."

Braley looked pointedly at his watch.

"He's been gone fifteen minutes," said the American. "If we were going to be arrested, it would have happened by now."

Charlie nodded agreement, having already reached the same conclusion.

"The table would have been the best spot," he enlarged. "During the conversation, his men could have got so close that we wouldn't have had a chance to blink."

"So we *aren't* going to be busted?" demanded Braley.

It was a hopeful question, recognised the Briton. He shrugged, unhelpfully. "How the hell do I know?"

They went through the archway and began to walk towards Wenceslaus Square.

"If they're going to arrest us, it won't really matter," said Charlie. "But I think we should immediately part to double the chances of what's been said getting back to London."

Braley nodded.

"If I manage to reach it, I'm going to remain in the embassy until the last possible moment for the flight," advised Charlie.

"Right," agreed Braley, enthusiastically.

"There's a flight at 1530 tomorrow, BE 693," listed Charlie. "Aim for that."

Charlie's walk back across the Charles Bridge to the embassy was a pleasant, relaxed meander. He ate alone in his room that night, drinking nothing and left the following day with just two hours to reach the airport, knowing the flight would have been called by the time he reached the departure lounge.

Braley was waiting for him aboard the aircraft, the asthma gradually subsiding.

"Well?" queried Charlie. "Now what do you think?"

"It doesn't make sense," said Braley. "It just doesn't make bloody sense."

"Good trip?" asked Edith.

"All right," agreed Charlie.

"Surprised you came straight home," said his wife, accusingly.

Charlie stared back at her, curiously. For several seconds she held his gaze, then looked away.

"There's been a reason every time I've been late home," he insisted. "You know that."

"So you keep telling me," she said, unconvinced.

"Don't be stupid," he said. He snapped his mouth shut. It would be wrong to argue with her, using her to relieve his nervousness, he thought.

She ignored the challenge.

"So it is definitely the nineteenth?" she said.

"Looks like it."

She looked directly at him again, the hostility gone.

"I'm frightened, Charlie," she said.

"So am I," said her husband. "Bloody frightened."

Kastanazy paused at the end of his account to the full Praesidium. There was no movement from the other fourteen men.

"And that, Comrades, would appear to be a full summation of the situation thus far," he said. No one believed him, he saw.

"Are you sure?" demanded the Party Secretary.

Kastanazy nodded.

"Incredible," judged Zemskov. "Absolutely incredible."

16

Cuthbertson would think of it as a war-room, thought Charlie, watching the British Director move around the office, indicator stick held loosely in his right hand. He had used it like a conductor leading a symphony orchestra all morning.

Charlie yawned, unable to conceal the fatigue. It had been a series of fifteen-hour days since their return from Czechoslovakia. After the combined report from him and Braley, Ruttgers had been withdrawn to Washington for final consultations with the Secretary of State and the President, and two special Cabinet meetings had been called at which Cuthbertson had given the complete details at the personal prompting of the Premier.

There had been a final, direct telephone liaison between the American leader and the Prime Minister and then joint approval given for the crossing plan devised by Cuthbertson and Ruttgers.

One hundred and fifty British and American operatives had already been drafted into Vienna and three tons of mobile electrical equipment flown in and housed at the American embassy. Fifty more men were being moved in that day.

In Cuthbertson's room, the map displacements had been completed. A gold flag marked Kalenin's crossing at Laa and then markers indicated his anticipated journey along the minor roads through Stronsdorf to Ernstbrunn, then to Korneuburg and into Vienna through Lagenzerdorf.

If there were pursuit, then the decoy car was to

ignore the Ernstbrunn turning and carry on towards Mistelbach. Separate coloured pins marked this contingency.

If the crossing went unchallenged, Kalenin would be brought to Vienna through a corridor of operatives, all linked by radio, so that they could close in behind, surrounding the Russian general in a circle of safety.

For two hours that morning, Cuthbertson and Ruttgers had stood before the map-table, lecturing on the crossing to the four section heads who were leaving that afternoon for the Austrian capital to co-ordinate the surveillance of the field operatives.

James Cox had already been withdrawn from Moscow and was in Vienna, waiting to be briefed on the decoy manœuvre he would perform on the Mistelbach road if the necessity arose.

Only the American section head knew about the explosive device and had been briefed in the privacy of the C.I.A. Director's Washington office before the Atlantic flight. The explosive package had been flown to Austria with the electronic equipment.

The section leaders had filed out fifteen minutes before, leaving the five of them in the room.

"All you've got to do," said Ruttgers, talking to Charlie, "is get him just one yard across that border; from then on there'll be no way it can go wrong."

Both he and Cuthbertson were hoarse with talking and it was Wilberforce who took up the discussion.

"Even so," he said, "we've been cornered at the conviction of both of you that there's still something wrong with this operation."

Charlie humped his shoulders, resigned.

"It's not a new feeling with me," he reminded them. "I've had doubts from the beginning."

"Which have so far proven groundless," rasped Cuthbertson.

"Harrison is dead and Snare insane," returned Charlie, immediately.

Cuthbertson reddened even more, annoyed at his error.

"It's not good about Snare," he admitted. "It'll go badly for him after Kalenin crosses."

"*If* he crosses," corrected Charlie. The Director didn't give a damn about Snare, Charlie knew. The whole project had become one of personal aggrandisement of himself and Ruttgers.

Ruttgers sighed, spreading his hands.

"For Christ's sake," he said, to both operatives. "What are you trying to say?"

"I agree with Charlie," offered Braley, helpfully. "There's not a thing I can prove, not a fact I can show to support the slightest doubt, yet I have the same misgivings."

Wilberforce looked up from his bony hands.

"But if anything were to have happened, it would have done so by now, surely?" asked the tall man, reasonably. "You were open, identifiable targets in Prague."

"I've still got to cross at Laa, to assure him everything is ready," reminded Charlie.

"That wouldn't make sense, to grab you there," rejected Wilberforce. "Why bother to trap one man when he had two in the Czech capital. And he could have had you arrested far easier in Moscow, weeks ago."

Charlie nodded.

"I know," he said, defeated.

"I think this is a pointless discussion," dismissed Cuthbertson. "Every proposal upon which we've decided has been assessed and analysed for faults. Any illogicality would have been thrown up. The only thing to result from further discussion will be confusion."

Charlie gestured reluctant agreement.

"So let's get to the last details," hurried Ruttgers, impatiently.

Again it was Wilberforce who spoke, addressing the two operatives.

"Kalenin said he didn't want a caravan of cars," he reminded. "So there'll just be you two in the lead Mercedes. In three other vehicles, about fifty yards back from the border, will be the resistance teams in case there is a pursuit, and the driver of the decoy car."

"What if Kalenin brings his own car across?" asked Braley.

"Transfer him immediately and leave it for disposal to the back-up team," instructed Wilberforce. "A Czech registered car will attract too much attention."

"There's no courtyard in the Wipplingerstrasse house," remarked Charlie, looking at a blown-up photograph of where they were going to conceal Kalenin.

"So?" asked Ruttgers.

"What happens if there is pursuit and your contingency plan doesn't work quite as smoothly as you expect it to? Our car could be spotted at the border and then become a marker in Wipplingerstrasse. If the Russians try to get him back, it'll be a blitz."

"Good point," praised Cuthbertson, reluctantly. "Once Kalenin is out of the vehicle in Wipplingerstrasse, move it away . . . hand it over to one of the back-up groups that will have travelled with you."

"What about border guards on the Austrian side?" persisted Braley.

"We've realised the importance of the time Kalenin stipulated," said Wilberforce. "Both sets of guards change duty at ten. The resistance team will look after the Austrian border officials and maintain the regular telephone liaison to ensure that nobody becomes suspicious until Kalenin is safely aboard the aircraft and on his way to London."

"How the hell do you avoid a diplomatic incident, immobilising border guards?" queried Charlie.

"We don't try," lectured Wilberforce. "The men who take out the Viennese posts will be dressed as Czech soldiers and speak Czech. The protests will involve Czechoslovakia, not us. There's no way we can be caught up."

"Unless the attack goes wrong."

"We've checked the border," insisted Wilberforce, irritated by the persistent argument. "At that time of night it'll be staffed by three men and nothing has happened at the border since 1968. They've grown sloppy."

"Will we have a radio link in the Mercedes?" asked Charlie.

"Yes," took up Cuthbertson, "obviously you will. But I don't think we should utilise it unless Kalenin needs any assurance that he's being well cared for."

"What about separation?" asked Braley.

Ruttgers smiled, an amateur magician with a favourite trick.

"Kalenin is obviously determined to have the money with him at all times," he reminded them. "The bag will have a transmitter concealed in the bottom, allowing us complete monitoring at all times."

"Seems everything has been considered," said Braley, sycophantically. Both Cuthbertson and Ruttgers smiled, appreciatively.

"Forty-eight hours from now," predicted Cuthbertson, "we'll be sitting in this office, celebrating the biggest intelligence coup of our lives."

"With Aloxe Corton?" asked Charlie, in soft sarcasm.

"What?" asked Wilberforce.

"Nothing," said Charlie, standing up and going over to the flagged and pinned map.

"All this, just for one man," he said, reflectively.

"Not just for any one man," corrected Cuthbertson. "A very special man."

"Yes," agreed Charlie, after a pause. "A very special man."

Charlie lay on his back in the darkness. Beside him he could just discern the smoke of Janet's cigarette.

"I'm sorry," he said.

"Don't be stupid," she answered, practically.

"It's never happened before," he complained.

"Keep on about it and you'll become permanently inpotent," said the girl. "With what you've got on your mind, what happened tonight is hardly surprising, is it?"

"Didn't happen," corrected Charlie.

The girl shifted position, annoyed again at the self-pity.

"I don't suppose the Director told you, did he?" she asked, obtusely.

"What?" said Charlie, disinterested.

"Sir Archibald Willoughby," said the girl. "He died while you and Braley were in Prague."

For several moments, there was silence in the room. There was no movement at all from Charlie.

"He was an alcoholic, apparently," offered the girl. "Been drinking for years."

"Not years," corrected Charlie, quietly. "Just about eighteen months. That's all."

"Anyway," accepted the girl. "Cause of death was cirrhosis of the liver."

"He was a very unhappy man," said Charlie, more to himself than to the girl. "I'm glad he's dead."

He felt her turn to him in the darkness.

"What an odd thing to say," she picked up. "How can you be glad anyone is dead?"

"I knew him very well," explained Charlie. "He really didn't want to live."

The girl moved, rising on one arm to grind out the cigarette and then twisting, so that she hovered over him. The tips of her breasts were brushing his chest but there was no sexual feeling between them.

"Be careful, Charlie," she said, worriedly.

"Of course."

"Don't be glib. I want you to come back."

It was several minutes before he replied.

"I'll come back," he guaranteed, finally.

Janet was glad the room was dark. She would have been embarrassed for him to see her cry again.

17

Charlie had protested about the danger of attracting attention, but Ruttgers and Cuthbertson, in complete and unified command now, had insisted on final rehearsals, actually driving to within a mile of the frontier along the winding, tree- and meadow-edged road to the Czech border and then back again, stop-watching the journey and testing the surveillance over every mile.

Satisfied, they had toured first by car and then on foot the streets surrounding the secure C.I.A. house in Wipplingerstrasse, isolating the watchers and ensuring each team had the necessary and prepared back-up group to move on any emergency radio command.

To the safe house the Directors had then summoned the section leaders for a final briefing. An American marine commander, Gordon Marshall, was controller of the resistance team at the crossing point. Another American, named Alton, was responsible for the route security into Vienna and a Briton, Arthur Byrbank, was co-ordinator for the journey to the airport. A British commando, Hubert Jessell, was to supervise the house and grounds.

The Directors agreed the placings were perfect and then took the four men through the entire operation, checking and cross-referring the codes and call signs until they were completely satisfied.

Neither Ruttgers nor Cuthbertson was going to allow the slightest possibility of error reflecting upon their personal involvement, decided Charlie, wryly, sitting near the window while the four section leaders received their final instructions.

It was a perfect house for the operation, apart from the absence of a courtyard in which to conceal the car, thought Charlie. It occupied its own grounds; tree-dotted and easily guarded, and secure behind an elec-tronically controlled gate opened by a command room console switch to a password known to only ten men.

The ground floor was given over to radio communi-cations and staffed by three men. The lounge in which they were now gathered and in which they intended to greet Kalenin was a huge, first-floor room, illuminated by chandeliers that hung from the high, vaulted ceil-ings. Despite the obvious cleaning, the faint, dusty smell of disuse still clung to the over-padded Viennese furniture which had been arranged in a loose circle around the table.

If the crossing went without incident, there was actu-ally talk of a snack meal before the flight to London, remembered Charie, amused.

At 6 P.M., the section heads left to get into position and Cuthbertson and Ruttgers were alone with the two operatives. The American Director was chain smoking; the occasional jerk in Cuthbertson's eye and the in-creased redness of his face were the only indications of his nervousness.

"Well," asked Cuthbertson, confidently.

"It was a mistake to have gone so completely over the route," criticised Charlie again, knowing Braley shared his view. "It created an unnecessary risk."

Ruttgers sighed. Increasingly, the C.I.A. Director found himself agreeing with the view that Cuthbertson had expressed: the Englishman was losing his nerve.

"It excluded the possibility of an error once the thing starts rolling," insisted the American.

"Or created it," argued Charlie.

"Are you frightened?" demanded Ruttgers, ag-gressively.

"Yes," came back Charlie. "Very frightened . . ." he paused. ". . . Only a fool wouldn't be frightened," he added, then concluded, pointedly, "or a psychopath."

Ruttgers jerked up at him, sharply, and Charlie answered the challenge. It was Ruttgers who looked away first.

Cuthbertson shifted, embarrassed at the hostility that had grown in the room.

"This isn't going to help the operation," he complained. "We're all on edge . . . bound to be. Let's make allowances, for God's sake . . ."

He moved to a side table and held up whisky.

"A drink, Charles," he suggested, immediately turning back. "Charlie," he corrected.

He was trying very hard, thought Charlie, sympathetically, watching the British Director pour quickly and then hurry the glasses to each man. The four of them stood embarrassed, like abandoned strangers at a party seeking conversation.

"To everything going well," toasted Cuthbertson, raising his glass.

Sir Archibald had usually given him a drink before the commencement of any operation, recalled Charlie. The hope had always been "a safe return."

He drank self-consciously, then looked pointedly at his watch, wanting to quit the company of men whom he despised.

"I think we should move," he said. "We can always stop en route if we make good time, but I don't want to be late."

Both Directors nodded agreement. It was going to be a diarrœtic four hours for them, thought Charlie, waiting alone in the lofty room with only sporadic radio messages to tell them what was happening.

Ruttgers stopped them at the door.

"Good luck," he said.

"And you, Charlie," pressed the American, smiling at his acceptance of the other man's affectation.

Charlie nodded, without replying, leading the way from the room.

Unchallenged, Charlie took the driver's seat and began moving the car along the now familiar route towards the Marien Bridge. Within fifteen minutes he had picked up the road to Langenzerdorf and had begun to relax. The traffic was comparatively light and it was a warm, dry evening with clouds, which would reduce the light during the cross-over. Perfect, thought Charlie.

As they passed each monitoring point, Braley depressed the code key on the radio, signalling their progress. Ruttgers and Cuthbertson would be in the control room now, guessed Charlie, charting their route on the map that had been laid out there.

"There's no reason why you should like them," said the American, after a while. "But equally there's no reason why you should be so rude."

"They're fools," judged Charlie.

"That's ridiculous and you know it," rejected Braley. "Fools can't hold down the positions they do."

Charlie shrugged, unwilling to pursue any argument. As they approached the border, Braley's breathing became more difficult, he noticed. When they got on the outskirts of Ernstbrunn, their radio clattered briefly as the units in Stockerau and Wolkersdorf identified themselves.

"It's working well," said Braley, nervously.

"Traps always do until they close around you," said Charlie, unhelpfully.

There was hardly any traffic on the road and they cleared Ernstbrunn in minutes. At the junction with the road to Mistelbach, Charlie slowed and then halted, knowing he was well ahead of time.

"It's a terrible road for a chase," he assessed, professionally.

Braley nodded agreement.

"I've been thinking that for miles," replied the American miserably. "Let's hope to Christ we can hold anything sufficiently long to make the decoy work."

Charlie looked sideways at him, questioningly.

"Just how far do you think the Russians and the

Czechs would go to get Kalenin back?" he demanded, rhetorically. "There's hardly a man in the Soviet Union more important to them. If they come, they'll cross that border like a steamroller, flattening everything in their path."

Braley slumped in his seat.

"Let's get going," he avoided. "I don't want to be late."

They reached the back-up cars, parked two miles from the border, at 9 P.M. Braley and Charlie stopped and crossed to the lead car, where Braley stared in momentary amazement at Cox sitting in the front seat.

"Jim," he exclaimed. "What the hell are you doing here?"

"Part of the team," said the athlete, happily. "Recalled from Moscow a week ago. I'm handling the decoy car. Think it'll work?"

"We hope so," replied Braley. He wondered what real diversion had been planned to involve Cox: certainly there would be no question of his getting captured. Poor bastard: still, he wasn't a very good operative.

Marshall, the section leader of the resistance group, was a crew-cut, taut man of sharp, abrupt movements. He sat alongside Cox, flexing and shrugging his shoulders, like a boxer limbering up before a bout. He's hoping there will be a chase, so he can involve himself in a fight, assessed Charlie.

"No last-minute snags?" demanded the Briton.

Marshall grinned sideways at the question, as if the idea were unthinkable.

"No last-minute snags," he echoed. He looked at the heavy Rolex watch that had been part of the élite snobbism of the Green Berets in Vietnam.

"The team are setting off in fifteen minutes to take out the border post," he reported.

"No one is to be killed," said Charlie, immediately. Marshall worried him, he decided. The marine was the sort of man who enjoyed killing.

"My men know what to do," snapped the American,

gazing at the unkempt Briton as if he'd trodden in dog droppings.

"They'd better," reminded Charlie, unperturbed. "The object is to avoid trouble, not cause it."

Marshall turned to look at him fully, his face inches away from Charlie's.

"You trying to tell me how to do it?" he demanded.

He would keep his voice very low because he would have read in books that it was how men spoke in such circumstances, thought Charlie. The marine's breath smelt of mint and he wore a heavy cologne, Charlie detected.

"No," he said, not moving his head away. "But if it becomes necessary, I shall. And I'll pull rank, gun or whatever other crap is necessary to ensure that my instructions are followed. The war in Asia, commander, is over. And your lot made muck of it."

The man's control was remarkable and Charlie was glad of it. There would have been no way he could have physically confronted him, Charlie knew.

The departure of the assault group broke the tension between them. Their faces were cork-blackened and they moved without sound. Complete experts, thought Charlie. And killers.

"I'll be in the lead car, fifty yards from the border," reported Cox, speaking to Braley.

The fat American nodded.

"If there's no chase, I shan't bother to stop. I'll leave you to follow automatically," Charlie told the marine commander.

Marshall nodded, tightly.

Charlie turned as Braley nudged him. The man was offering the luminous dial of his wristwatch to him.

"Time to go."

His breathing was very bad now, Charlie realised.

The Briton let himself quietly out of the car, returned to the Mercedes and sat for several seconds, hands gripping the wheel.

"You all right?" asked Braley, worried.

Charlie released a long sigh, then started the car.

"Yes," he said. "I'm fine."

"That was unnecessary, back there," said Braley, nodding over his shoulder to the car where Marshall sat.

"I know," conceded Charlie, embarrassed now.

"Then why do it?"

Charlie shrugged in the darkness.

"You've got to buck everyone, haven't you, Charlie?"

The Briton said nothing. It *had* been bloody stupid.

"You shouldn't do it, Charlie. There's no need for you to keep proving yourself."

"Forget it," said Charlie, irritated.

Braley stopped talking, looking sadly at the Englishman, and they made the two-mile drive enclosed in their separate fears. The road bent immediately before the border and Charlie stopped just short, so that the car was hidden. Braley's protest in Prague had been right, thought Charlie. Despite the clouds, it was hardly dark.

"Let's check on foot," he suggested.

They got carefully from the car, easing the doors open so there was no sound. Charlie led, keeping against the bank where the shadows were deepest. He'd moved like this with Snare he recalled, all those months ago in Berlin. And there'd been a trap for him at the border. And now Snare was mad.

The Austrian border post was completely quiet. Through the window of the tiny office, they could see one of Marshall's assault group. The man sat next to a telephone that kept liaison between the stations. He appeared relaxed and very comfortable.

"Do you think they'll have killed the guards?" asked Charlie.

"Yes," said Braley, immediately. As if it were justification, he offered: "It's the only way they're trained."

Charlie looked beyond the post, across the twenty yards of no-man's-land and into Czechoslovakia. There was no sign of activity from the communist side.

"We'll drive up," decided Charlie.

He took the car slowly, stopping against the customs office and dowsing the lights.

"It's too quiet," started Braley, worriedly, staring through the barriers.

"We're three minutes ahead of time," reminded Charlie.

Inside the customs post the telephone rang and one of Marshall's commandos answered, the dialect perfectly modulated. Ruttgers and Cuthbertson had considered every detail, conceded Charlie, listening to the exchange. The telephone call was a routine time check and the receiver was replaced within seconds. Beside him, Braley was dragging breath into his lungs, his shoulders rising and falling with the effort.

"Come on!" demanded the American, gazing over the border, hands clenched against his knees. "Come on!"

Charlie checked his watch.

"10:35," he recorded.

"Shall I radio the delay?" enquired Braley, quickly.

"It will have been done already," soothed Charlie. "If *we* make contacts as well, it will create panic."

"Where is the bloody man?" asked Braley, irritably.

"There," responded Charlie, pulling forward in his seat.

Two hundred yards across the border, a set of headlights had flashed, once. It was not possible to discern the outline of a car.

"What now?" asked Braley. His voice was uneven, the words jumping from him.

Charlie sat momentarily uncertain. The lights flickered on again, briefly.

"I go across," said the Briton, simply.

He tried to get quietly from the car, but this time the sound of the door opening seemed to echo in the quiet night. From the back seat he hauled the bugged moneybag, hefted it in his right hand and looked briefly back into the vehicle.

"See you in a few moments," predicted Charlie.

The men in the border posts were watching him,

Charlie knew, as he began to walk towards the barrier; the signal indicating contact would have already been flashed by one of Marshall's men to the secluded house in Wipplingerstrasse. He wondered what Cuthbertson and Ruttgers were doing.

Around him the sounds of the night chattered and rustled and he started looking into the darkness ahead, trying to detect movement. It was a warm, mellow evening: ideal for walking, reflected Charlie. At the Austrian barrier he paused, then ducked beneath it. He hadn't realised the money would weigh so heavily. He stopped, transferring it to the other hand. It was the unexpected weight of the bag that had made his hand shake, he decided.

"Keep cool, Charlie," he advised himself. "Don't ruin it all now."

He could make out the outline of a car, a small, inconspicuous shape half hidden by the Czech border installation. Barbed wire stretched from either side of the barrier posts and he could just identify the triangular shapes of tank obstructions. There would be mines, guessed Charlie, and electronic sensors. Just like East Berlin.

At the Czech barrier, he stood still, right hand resting on the pole. The shaking had stopped, he saw, gratefully. The impatient light burst from the darkened car, urging him on.

He hesitated several seconds, then ducked beneath it. The Czech border posts were completely deserted, he saw, yellow lights pooling into empty rooms. Beyond the control houses, he walked through a cathedral of tall pines which made it completely dark. It was still and quiet, like a church, he thought, extending his metaphor.

Gradually the whiteness of a face registered through the windscreen of the car he was approaching and when he got nearer he saw the figure move, winding down the driver's window.

"You appear very nervous, Mr. Muffin," greeted Kalenin.

"Yes," agreed Charlie.

The General got from the car, smiling up at him. He opened his coat, disclosing civilian clothes.

"I had intended to wear my uniform and medals," he said, calmly. "But then I decided it might have created difficulties in Vienna."

"Yes," said Charlie, "it might have done."

Around them the night was wrapped like a blanket. There was no sound from the forest, realised Charlie, suddenly. Which was wrong. There should have been animal movement, as there was on the Austrian side.

"I've a great many medals," said Kalenin.

"I know," said Charlie.

The Russian nodded towards the bag.

"Is that the money?"

Charlie lifted it onto the hood of the car.

"Yes," he said.

"I suppose I should examine it?"

"Yes," said Charlie. "It was bloody heavy carrying it all this way."

Kalenin unsnapped the fastenings and ruffled the notes.

"So much money," he said, whimsically.

"Enough for a lifetime," assessed Charlie.

Kalenin jerked his head back across the border.

"They'll be watching through infra-red nightglasses," he guessed.

"Yes," said Charlie. "The advance party will have them. The message will have already been sent to Vienna that we've met."

Kalenin nodded. He seemed reluctant to move, thought Charlie.

"The whole border seems deserted," pressed Charlie.

"Yes," said Kalenin, easily. "I've got great power in all the satellite countries. Whatever I say is obeyed. It was really very easy."

Charlie looked back into Austria.

"There's a man back there who hoped you'd be pursued by armed guards," he reported.

"Sometimes I feel sorry for the Americans," said

Kalenin. "There's so many who'd like still to go West in covered wagons, shooting Indians."

The two men stood for several seconds looking at each other.

"Well," said Kalenin, finally, "shall we go?"

"Yes," said Charlie.

"I think I should carry the money," said Kalenin, reaching out.

"Of course," agreed Charlie.

Wilberforce remained on duty in the Whitehall office, waiting for the message from Vienna that Kalenin was on his way. He had delayed until late in the evening seeing Janet, hoping a signal would make the encounter impossible, but no contact had been made and now he sat gazing down into his lap, embarrassed by the completeness of the girl's account of the previous night. He'd already listened to the recordings of the tapes of which she was unaware and knew she had omitted nothing. Involving her had been an offensive mistake, decided Wilberforce.

"In many ways," he said, apologetically, "I regret the decision to ask you to inform upon the man. It's proved completely unnecessary. And distasteful."

"I know," said Janet.

Wilberforce looked up at her and for the first time she realised how pale his eyes were. They gave his face an unreal, frightening expression.

He smiled, kindly.

"You've grown very fond of him, haven't you?" he probed.

"Yes," admitted Janet, immediately, "which makes what I've done even worse."

"You'll have to get over it, you know," advised the civil servant. "Nothing can possibly come of any relationship."

"I know," accepted the secretary.

She moved forward in her chair.

"Tell me," she demanded, "he'll be all right, after

this, won't he? I mean the Director won't dump him, like he was planning to, all those months ago."

Wilberforce took several minutes to reply.

"I don't know," he lied, finally.

The telephone made them both jump.

"They've met," reported Wilberforce, replacing the receiver. "Kalenin and Charlie have met."

18

"It's very heavy," complained Kalenin, as they approached the Austrian border.

"Shall I help?"

"I think I can manage," said the General, using two hands to hold the case. The tiny Russian paused before the barrier, lowering the bag to the ground.

"The moment of commitment," he said, turning to Charlie.

"Yes," agreed the Briton.

Kalenin sighed, then positively shoved the bag beneath the post with his foot. It grated over the road, an irritating, scratching sound.

"Too late to go back now," he said.

"Yes," said Charlie. "I thought that on the way over."

They bent together beneath the bar and walked easily towards the Mercedes. Braley had turned the car, Charlie saw. He would have expected to have heard the sound of the engine.

Marshall was in the border post now, Charlie noticed, gazing hopefully over their shoulders for pursuit. His men would be developed on either side of the road, Charlie knew. They were very professional: it was impossible to isolate them against the blackness of the woods.

Charlie escorted the Russian past the point without looking, suddenly anxious to get away from the area. Braley was waiting, the car doors already open.

"I'll travel in the front," selected Kalenin. He turned to Charlie.

"Are you the driver?"

"Yes," said Charlie.

The Russian nodded, as if the information were important.

Braley held the door for him and Kalenin seated himself fussily, arranging his coat comfortably about him before lowering the case on to his lap.

Charlie and the American paused briefly, looking at each other. Then Braley closed the door and Charlie hurried to the driver's seat.

He started badly, accelerating too quickly and felt Kalenin's eyes upon him. Charlie gripped the wheel and slowed, staring at the twisting road.

"A pleasant evening," remarked Kalenin, conversationally.

"Yes," said Braley, after waiting for Charlie to respond. "Very pleasant, sir."

Charlie reached the Ernstbrunn turning and came off the road to Mistelbach. On the highway far behind he could just detect the lights of the cars returning Marshall and his unhappy commandos.

"I'm glad there was no trouble, sir," tried Braley embarrassed by the silence in the car.

"I was confident there wouldn't be," said Kalenin immediately. "If I decree a border post remain unmanned, then it is unmanned."

The lights of Korneuburg fireflied in front. The teams at Stockerau and Wolkersdorf would have already been informed that it had been a quiet crossing and be moving in to cover him, Charlie knew. And Marshall's cars were quite close behind now. The protection was complete.

"We're well guarded?" queried Kalenin, presciently.

"Utterly protected," assured Charlie. "It would be impossible to stop us now."

"What about a routine Austrian police patrol?"

"They would only want my driver's documents," said Charlie. "And they're in order."

Langenzerdorf was deserted and they were on the outskirts of Vienna in the time that Ruttgers and Cuthbertson had estimated during their trial run. They crossed the Danube canal and passed the post office, turning right into Fleischmarktstrasse to get into the old part of the city. Over the rooftops, he could see the spire of St. Stephen's Cathedral. It looked very peaceful, thought Charlie.

Every unit would be on full alert now; and Ruttgers and Cuthbertson would have quit the first floor lounge and be in the radio room, he guessed, charting their progress street by street.

He turned slowly into Wipplingerstrass. Marshall's team had stopped at the junction behind him, blocking it until the Russian had entered the house.

"Escort the General in," said Charlie. "I'll take the car on."

The American left the car and opened Kalenin's door. The tiny Russian got out immediately and stopped, waiting for Braley's lead. The secured gate opened the moment the American spoke into the grill. Subserviently, he allowed Kalenin to lead as they went along the darkened pathway. The door was opened by Hubert Jessell as Braley knocked. The American led up the stairway, the breath squeaking from him.

The lounge door was already open, light shafting into the corridor.

Ruttgers and Cuthbertson stood side by side, the table separating them from the Russian. Braley entered and then closed the door, standing directly inside. For several seconds, no one spoke, apparently unable to believe the crossing had gone so well.

Ruttgers recovered first, hurrying around the table, hand outstretched.

"General," he greeted. "Welcome! Welcome indeed."

Kalenin smiled at the greeting, accepting his hand.

"You must be . . . ?" he invited.

"Ruttgers," identified the C.I.A. Director. "Garson Ruttgers. And allow me to introduce my English counterpart, General Sir Henry Cuthbertson."

The Briton had followed him around the table, hand held forward.

"A pleasure, General," assured Cuthbertson. "A very great pleasure."

Kalenin shrugged off his topcoat and held it awkwardly. Immediately Braley was at his arm, taking it.

Ruttgers took the Russian by the elbow, moving him further into the room.

"A perfect crossing," congratulated Cuthbertson. "A copybook operation."

"I have the necessary power," reminded Kalenin, modestly.

"A drink," suggested Cuthbertson. "I think a celebration is in order."

"I enjoy your Scotch whisky very much," accepted Kalenin, hopefully. "And I agree, we've got something to celebrate."

Ruttgers and Cuthbertson were tight with excitement, each aware of the incredible prestige of their coup. The Briton over-filled the glasses, only remembering Braley as an after-thought.

"We had taken every precaution to ensure nothing would interfere on this side," guaranteed Ruttgers, eager to boast.

"A plane is waiting, at Schwechat," added Cuthbertson. "We'll be safely in London by dawn tomorrow."

From the communications centre below, notification of Kalenin's safe arrival had already been sent to Wilberforce and Downing Street. By now, guessed Cuthbertson, a personal telephone call would have been made by the Premier to the American President.

"Your health," toasted Kalenin, raising his glass.

"And yours," responded Ruttgers, sincerely.

Kalenin moved to one of the more comfortable chairs arranged around the table.

"It was important that you came personally to greet me," he said, to both Directors.

"It's unthinkable that we would not come," replied Ruttgers.

Kalenin sipped the drink, appearing quite relaxed.

"Tell me your plans," he ordered.

"There is accommodation waiting in England," reported Cuthbertson. "Four completely safe houses in each of which you'll live from time to time."

"It will be a long process," suggested Kalenin. Apparently reminded of time, he looked at his watch.

"Yes," agreed Ruttgers. "But during it you will live in absolute luxury and complete safety. Your security will be a joint American–British responsibility."

"Of course," said Kalenin.

"We've taken every step to ensure your comfort," expanded Cuthbertson. He smiled, a man about to produce the best present at a party.

"You enjoy war-games with tanks, I believe?" he asked.

Kalenin frowned, then nodded.

"They've been provided for you, at every house," smiled the English Director.

"That was very thoughtful of you."

"We are anxious that you will be completely happy ... we've complied with your every request so far ..."

"Indeed," said Kalenin. "I've been very grateful."

He looked pointedly at his empty glass and Cuthbertson moved immediately to fill it.

"As soon as you feel sufficiently rested," said Ruttgers, "perhaps it would be a good idea if we were to get to the airport."

Kalenin nodded, without replying, the glass held before his face with both hands.

"You created a remarkable operation," said the Russian, at last.

"Thank you," said Ruttgers.

". . . the road all the way to Schwechat covered, this entire area from the canal to the city hall and Am Hof Square, right down to the riding school and the Volksgarten . . ."

Ruttgers nodded, content with the praise. His voice was strained by the smoking and he coughed, frequently.

". . . and then the border organisation, with teams at Stockerau and Wolkersdorf, Ernstbrunn and Korneuburg . . ."

Ruttgers began staring at the Russian, curiously.

"How . . . ?" he began, but Kalenin shook his head, imperiously. Again he looked at his watch.

"It's been an hour and thirty minutes since I arrived in Vienna," the Russian declared, smiling.

Both Directors were looking at him now, baffled.

"Time enough," completed Kalenin.

"General," tried Cuthbertson, hopefully, "I'm sorry, but . . ."

". . . you don't understand," finished Kalenin. There was a tone in his voice now, a man in control.

Reluctantly he placed his empty glass on the table.

"Excellent whisky," he praised, turning to them and smiling. "No, there's no possible way that you could . . ."

He looked carefully from Cuthbertson to the American and then back again.

"Over a year ago," he said addressing Cuthbertson, "you British broke a Soviet espionage chain . . . it was remarkable for you to have done so. We thought of it as a brilliant installation, virtually undetectable. That you *did* uncover it was extremely damaging for us . . . and personally embarrassing to me . . ."

Both Directors were quite still: Cuthbertson had his head bent to one side, as if he had difficulty in hearing. His face was deepening in colour and his eye was fluttering.

"Moscow regarded the system created by Alexei Berenkov as the best in Europe since the war . . ."

From where Braley stood there was an uncomfortable movement of scuffing feet.

". . . Now Berenkov is in jail. And you both know that Russia does not allow its operatives, particularly one so highly regarded as Berenkov, to remain in captivity longer than is absolutely essential . . ."

". . . Are you telling us . . ." attempted Ruttgers, but again Kalenin cut him off.

". . . I'm telling you that the Soviet government, which has already, incidentally, established a service to replace that which was broken, decided to repatriate

Berenkov as soon as possible and deal to the espionage services of the West as damaging a blow as possible, to compensate for the destruction of Berenkov's network."

He stopped, waiting, but now neither Ruttgers nor Cuthbertson spoke.

"Within the last ninety minutes," recounted the Russian General, "my men have seized, I sincerely hope without any fighting, the 200 operatives that you had positioned to guard my crossing . . ."

". . . But that's impossible!" protested Cuthbertson.

"Oh no, not at all," disagreed Kalenin. "All you need is organisation and the right information, and I've got both. But I anticipated you would find it difficult to accept. I'm now in complete charge of this house. No doubt you've a method for summoning your people. Try it . . ."

Cuthbertson jabbed at a button set into the table, prodding it impatiently for response. They remained waiting for several minutes, but no one came.

"Oh my God," muttered Cuthbertson.

". . . But that means . . ." realised Ruttgers, unwilling to complete the fear.

". . . that as well as your operatives, I intend taking back to the Soviet Union for barter the English and American security Directors," confirmed Kalenin, happily.

"As I explained," he enlarged, "we decided to make it as damaging as possible. Of course, we'll release you both, in exchange for Berenkov. And all your operatives, too. They will be useless, unfortunately, photographed, fingerprinted and identified. But at least you'll have them back . . ."

He hesitated, preparing the blow.

"And you'll both be utterly discredited," he added. "The whole operation will set your services back years."

"What you've outlined would be impossible," insisted Cuthbertson, laughing nervously. "So few people knew the complete operation . . ."

His voice broke away and he looked beyond Kalenin to where only Braley stood.

"Yes," concurred the Russian, seeing the gradual realisation. "There was no way I could have evolved the thing by myself."

"Jesus!" exclaimed Ruttgers.

"You really were incredibly stupid, Sir Henry. Charlie Muffin was one of the few real operatives in your service. Yet you set him up to be shot in Berlin, vilified him for his handling of the Berenkov affair when it was he who originated and co-ordinated the capture and then announced he was being downgraded . . ."

Kalenin spread his hands, in mock exasperation.

"How can you expect loyalty when you treat a man like that?" he demanded.

"The bastard," shouted Ruttgers.

"Yes," agreed Kalenin. "But he never made the pretence of being anything else, did he?"

"You don't think we'll let you get out of this room alive?" demanded Ruttgers, desperately defiant.

The Russian frowned, irritated.

"Mr. Ruttgers," he protested, mildly, "this room is the only one in the house not occupied by men, all of whom are armed. Not that their weapons really matter. They'll be through that door exactly two seconds after I give the command. I agree you could probably shoot me in that time, but to what point? At the moment, my country is prepared to deal with this matter in the utmost secrecy. But if I die, every detail will be leaked to the West, before your repatriation. That wouldn't make for a very pleasant homecoming to Washington, would it?"

"We'll still be laughing-stocks," said Ruttgers, deflated.

"I'm afraid so," accepted the Russian. "But only to a few people in your governments. And you'll be alive."

"What about the money?" demanded Cuthbertson, suddenly.

"Oh, yes," said Kalenin, reminded. "That's Charlie's. Don't forget he's got a long retirement and he's forfeited his pension rights."

"I'll get him," vowed Ruttgers. "If it takes me until the day I die, I'll get him."

"He expects you might try," said Kalenin. "I don't think he's too worried."

He felt in his pocket.

"He thought you might want this back," he said to Ruttgers, extending the device the American had installed in the bottom of the money-bag.

"Not that it would really have mattered," added the Russian. "You've no one for a hundred miles you could have employed to trace it."

Kalenin stood, shouting a command as he rose. Braley remained stolidly in front of the door, awaiting instructions.

Ruttgers tensed, then sighed, his shoulders drooping. He shook his head impatiently and the fat American unlocked it.

"Shall we go?" invited Kalenin.

19

Charlie and Edith sat cross-legged on the floor, the money piled neatly before them. Charlie held the list of numbered notes he and Braley had created and was carefully removing those that were a danger to them. Edith sat nearer the fire, feeding the money into the flames.

"Fifty thousand," she moaned. "It seems such a waste!"

Would she ever lose her concern for money? wondered Charlie.

"We'll have to be very careful," he warned. "Both Ruttgers and Cuthbertson are vindictive sods. It'll all have to go."

"Are you really worried, darling?" asked his wife.

Charlie paused in his selection, considering the question.

"Properly aware of the dangers," he said, firmly.

"You've got more money than me now, Charlie," said the woman, in sudden realisation. The barrier would be down between them, at last. She was glad, she decided.

Charlie smiled at her, content with her admission.

"I know," he said. The satisfaction was very obvious in his voice.

"Why don't we spend mine first? I cashed all the shares and drew the money out, as you asked. Let's get rid of my damned inheritance."

Charlie looked at her, aware of the sacrifice. Edith was embarking completely upon a new life, he thought.

He hadn't known she'd appreciated so fully the resentment he had always felt about her wealth.

"Yes," he agreed. "That would keep us going for several years, without having to touch this."

He patted the bricks of money lying on the floor, then stood up, stretching the cramp from his legs.

"I never thought it would work, Charlie, when you told me why we were going on holiday after East Berlin and the Berenkov trial. I really didn't," she said.

"No," agreed Charlie, gazing through the window and watching the incoming tide throw pebbles up on to the beach. "There were times when I was doubtful."

"I'm amazed you and Kalenin were able to cover every eventuality from that one set of meetings in Austria."

"Kalenin is brilliant," praised Charlie. "It was his idea to bring in the Americans, knowing that Washington's presence would occupy Cuthbertson so much initially that any flaws we hadn't covered would have more chance of going unnoticed. Kalenin had a personality file on Ruttgers and guessed exactly how the American would behave. He and Cuthbertson were too worried thinking about each other to properly consider what I was doing . . ."

"Didn't you ever make a mistake?" asked his wife, admiringly.

"Not really a mistake," conceded Charlie. "Kalenin was anxious Berenkov should know he'd not been forgotten and that offers were being made to get him out. So during a meeting with Berenkov in Wormwood Scrubs, months ago, I had to mention Kalenin's name before I was supposed to have known about it. I sweated for days that it would be spotted on analysis, but it wasn't."

He stopped, reflecting Edith's question.

"And then," he continued, "during the first meeting with Cuthbertson, I got worried at one stage that I was being too convincing with the doubts about Kalenin's defection. I got away with it, though. They might have doubted my courage, but never my loyalty."

"*Don't* you feel guilty?" seized the woman.

"No," he insisted, positively. "There was hardly a meeting when I didn't warn them there was something wrong. I repeated it until they were tired of hearing it . . ."

". . . which was the entire psychology of doing it," rejected Edith, ". . . and to salve your own conscience . . ."

"Perhaps," said Charlie. "But I'm not sorry to have disgraced Cuthbertson. He'll have to retire, which means another Director. And that can only result in good for the service. Wilberforce will still be there to ensure continuity. I don't like him, but at least he understands the system!"

"I can't believe you don't feel any guilt," persisted Edith. "You betrayed your country."

"I rid the service of a man who was bound to lead it to disaster."

"That's a personal justification."

"And exposed to every Western intelligence system the identity of Kalenin, who had been a mystery for thirty years."

"And got a fortune in return," she said.

"The service had abandoned me," insisted Charlie. "It's better than growing roses on a Grade IV pension and being pissed by three o'clock every afternoon."

Edith shook her head. He would feel ashamed, in the future, she knew. Would it create another barrier? she thought, worriedly. They only had each other, now.

"I'm going to enjoy being able to afford good clothes," reflected Charlie. "And keeping a decent wine bin."

He looked down at his scuffed Hush Puppies. He'd keep them as a souvenir, he decided.

"You always were a snob, Charlie," protested his wife, laughing at him.

"But honest about it," he defended, "always honest."

"Why *did* you have to be so scruffy?"

"Psychology," avoided Charlie. "It made them contemptuous of me. People never respect a person of whom they're contemptuous."

And it would have meant using even more of your money, he added, mentally.

"Don't you feel sorry about Harrison and Snare?"

He frowned. Why was Edith so determined there should be some contrition? he wondered.

"Those two bastards stood on a viewing platform in Berlin, watching for me either to get captured or shot. When I got to the Kempinski, they were celebrating my death. Why should I feel sorry for them?"

Edith shuddered, very slightly.

"You don't forget, do you, Charlie? Ever?"

"No," he accepted. "Never."

His wife stared at him for several minutes, uncertain whether to raise the question. Then she said, hurriedly: "Was it really necessary to have an affair with that secretary?"

"Essential," said Charlie. "It deflected their interest away from you completely . . . made it possible for you finally to draw all the money out without their thinking of checking your account. When they bugged her apartment, which I didn't expect, it gave me a channel to feed Cuthbertson any attitude I wished. And from Janet I got everything I wanted to know about their thinking."

She sat, unconvinced.

"With Janet," persisted Charlie, "they thought they had a trap on every unguarded moment. Through her and the recorders, I was able to prove myself and allay any suspicion before it had time to arise."

"Poor Janet," said Edith, sadly.

"Forget it," advised Charlie. "There was no feeling. It was a game for her, like backgammon or Scrabble. And I bet she made some money, as well."

"It seems a daft thing to say in the circumstances, Charlie, but I hope you're right. I don't like to think of you being cruel."

"It was a necessary part of survival," said Charlie.

"Promise me you never loved her?"

"I promise," said Charlie, looking up and smiling directly at his wife.

"Will they be searching for us now, Charlie?"

The man nodded.

"Bound to be," he said. "But knowing their minds they will think of the Mediterranean. Or perhaps the Far East. Certainly not here, in Brighton."

"I do hope it's a nice summer," said Edith, going to the window. "I did so much like to travel."

"I gave you a holiday of a lifetime before contacting Kalenin," reminded Charlie. "And we'll do it again, in a few years' time."

"Kiss me, Charlie," said Edith, urgently. "Kiss me and say you love me."

He crawled across the floor, dislodging the money from the orderly piles, and embraced his wife.

"I *do* love you, Edith," he said.

"And I love you, Charlie. I was very worried, you know."

"Worried?"

"That you'd leave me for her."

Charlie frowned, his face inches from hers.

"But why should I have done that?"

"It's just that sometimes you frighten me, Charlie . . . we've been married fifteen years and there are times when I think of you as a stranger."

"That's a point," he said, pulling away and wanting to lighten the mood. "I'll have to get another name."

"But Charlie is so . . . I don't know. It just seems to fit," she protested.

"Not any more," insisted the man. He squatted, reflectively. He would take the Christian name of the old Director, he decided.

"It will be Archibald," he announced, grandly. "I'll keep the first name, but from now on it will be Charles."

What a pity that Cuthbertson would never know, he thought. He rolled the words uncomfortably in his mouth.

"Charles Archibald," he declared. "With a very defi-
nite accent on the 'Charles'. Charlie Muffin is dead."

The Home Office car drove directly on to the airstrip,
ten minutes after the rest of the passengers had
boarded BE 602 to Moscow.

Berenkov got unsteadily from the vehicle and stood
for several minutes, supported by one of the officials,
gazing for the last time at the Heathrow complex. Finally he turned and shuffled with difficulty up the steps
and into the specially curtained first class section.

The steward approached him after they had cleared
the airport and the seat-belt sign had been turned off.

"A drink, sir?" he suggested.

Berenkov looked up, whey-face, considering the invitation.

"It's been so long," he said, quietly. "So very long."

The steward waited.

"You'd only have claret in those little bottles, of
course," said the Russian, professionally. "And that
wouldn't be what I'd enjoy. I'll have a miniature champagne."

He watched apprehensively as the drink foamed in
the glass, then waited for the bubbles to settle.

Finally he lifted it, then paused, glass almost to his
lips.

"Your health, Charlie Muffin," he said.

"Sir?" enquired the steward, half turning.

"Nothing," said Berenkov. "Nothing at all."